VIOLET

VIOLET

Rachel LaCroix

authorHOUSE®

AuthorHouse™
1663 Liberty Drive
Bloomington, IN 47403
www.authorhouse.com
Phone: 1-800-839-8640

First published by AuthorHouse   10/19/2011

ISBN: 978-1-4670-7193-2 (sc)
ISBN: 978-1-4670-7192-5 (ebk)

Library of Congress Control Number: 2011919101

Printed in the United States of America

Any people depicted in stock imagery provided by Thinkstock are models, and such images are being used for illustrative purposes only. Certain stock imagery © Thinkstock.

This book is printed on acid-free paper.

Acknowledgments

I would like to thank my family for always supporting me while I worked on *Violet*. I would also like to thank Parrain Greg, my mom, and my English teachers and a very special librarian for reading my story first and giving me helpful suggestions, along with all of my middle school teachers for supporting me and always telling me to follow my dreams. I would also like to thank my friends, new and old, for being excited and putting up with me as I went on and on about how excited I was for finally getting published, and for Authorhouse, for helping me reach my dreams early in life. And lastly, I would like to thank you, the reader, for taking the time to read about the world through Violet's eyes. You guys rock!

Introduction

The world is a cruel, unfaithful place. Some believe that greed, lust, money, and the hunger for power is the reason why the world is what it is. But the people who think that those are the reasons are wrong. The real reason is because of human nature.

Yes, the world is coming to an end because humans have brought it upon themselves from simply being a human. They think they can survive anything. They can't. They need protection from the upcoming apocalypse.

I think that's probably the reason Severin and I was created in the first place.

Chapter One

"It's a success!" the worker cried as the boy opened his eyes. I stood watch from the other side of the room, strapped to the same type of bed as the boy.

I sighed. *That poor boy* I thought to myself. One moment, he's lying near death in the hospital, and the next, he's strapped to a laboratory bed in a new place with all of these strange things added to his body. He'll be a freak—just like me.

Well, at least now I'm not alone.

I was a human once. I think I might have had great life with a mom, dad, and maybe a little brother or sister—until I was kidnapped by these people who transformed my life—physically. Now instead of cuddling up with a boyfriend, I am sitting in a sterile white room watching as the people who took my life away create a mate for me.

Yeah, you heard me right. They created this boy to be like me—scaly torso, bat like wings attached to the back, small horns poking out of the head, and retractable claws on the hands and feet—to be my mate. So they don't have to spend money making more of me.

The boy looked around at the rejoicing doctors with a frightened glance. He began to pull against the bonds attached to him. Then his body began to shake with the high powered electric shocks coursing through his veins from the restraints.

Yeah, you don't want to do that I thought at him silently. I learned about the shocks the hard way too.

"Come now, Severin, we will not hurt you," said one of the workers gently to him, untying the bonds.

So Severin was his name, huh?

Severin seemed to be contemplating whether or not he could trust him.

Once he was released from the bonds that held him down, he, unsurprisingly, tried to escape. The blanket that covered his bottom half slipped away, revealing some stuff on him that I really wish I hadn't seen. I turned my head when the workers started to shock him with their sticks. Excited chatter and commotion filled the room. *God, why is it so loud?* I asked myself, wincing at the noise of Severin's cries of pain as the shocks began to petrify him. After a few minutes, he slumped to the floor.

I looked to find the workers gently picking him up and bringing him out the door. One worker named Aaron stayed to untie me. "Now, Violet, will you be a good girl to Severin?" he asked in a polite voice. I didn't answer. His expression turned sour. "I know you are only five weeks old, but you have responsibilities to take care of, now that you are a mutant."

"Oh, so you still don't have a name for my species?" I shot at him. His eyes narrowed. "Don't play games with me, Violet," he said threateningly, untying me from the bed.

"So, tell me again why you made me witness the life come back into some boy I don't even know," I said, my voice laced with sarcasm. He sighed impatiently. "We thought you might want to see your new mate come to life," he said softly.

I groaned. "Why would I want to go off and have kids with a guy I don't even know?" Now he looked really annoyed. He grabbed my now free hands and began to lead me back to my cage.

Well, more like a dog crate with a window.

We walked down the sterile white hallway that lead to the cages, testing rooms, training rooms, and rooms filled with torture devices in case I disobeyed.

We reached my wooden cage (dog crate) when we heard this awful, inhuman scream that scared the living daylights out of me and Aaron. "What the hell was that?" I practically

3

shouted. Aaron shook his head, his bouncy brown locks shifting from side to side. "I don't know. Get inside and stay there," he said, motioning me inside the crate. I was barely able to crawl inside when he locked the cage door and made a bolt for the exit.

Then there was only the silence I was so used to hearing. I sighed. Splinters stung into my bare hands and feet as I lay on them. Darkness surrounded me, making me think that Hell had broken loose and covered the world in eternal night. The smell of the last mutant that lived here lingered in the crate walls.

Suddenly, the door swung open to reveal a limp Severin in the arms of Aaron walking towards me. The world outside of the door revealed chaos like a battlefield in motion. The cries of workers could be heard as glass shattered in the testing room. I even could have sworn there were death cries right before I heard loud thumps like a body hitting the floor. But for some reason, I wasn't all that afraid. Actually, I kind of liked the new action taking place.

Aaron laid Severin down as he grabbed his keys and quickly unlocked my door. "Get out, and quickly!" he said, swinging open my door and pulling me out by the hands. The sudden brightness of the lights hurt my eyes momentarily, but I immediately adjusted. I stumbled to my feet as Aaron picked up Severin and grabbed my arm. I was just about to make a break for it to the door when Aaron pulled me into another direction.

"What the hell are you doing?" I asked. "The door is that way."

"We are taking another way out," he said, and he put his pale hand on the wall. Without warning, a secretly concealed door appeared on the wall! Blue and purple electricity crackled around it, as if it was a movie prop that might disappear.

"Get inside this door, and don't come out until I come to get you," he said, a hint of desperation in his voice. He almost literally threw me and Severin into the surprisingly large, windowless room on the other end of the door with only a small light bulb to light up the room. I landed on my stomach with a painful "oomph!" as Aaron closed the door on us, leaving an unconscious Severin and me to wait in the dimly lit secret hideout.

Chapter Two

Pain shot through my limbs as I sat up and struggled to breathe. Man, that fall had really knocked the breath out of me! After several long, painful minutes, I was finally able to breathe normally again. I looked to my right to find Severin beginning to stir. He was lying down on his stomach, with his arms cushioning his fall. His thick, strait black hair sat on his head, hiding his newly borne horns, and I was close enough to see a small freckle on the tip of his nose. His eyelids fluttered, and then opened slowly.

He had the softest blue eyes I had ever seen. They had a surprising depth that could make one feel as if she was drowning into an unknown abyss. Any girl would fall to their knees if they saw them.

Too bad I'm not one of them.

He blinked and shot into a sitting position, which complimented his lean yet slightly muscular body. "Where am I?" he asked me, his voice like soft velvet in his distress.

I chuckled. "With me," I said, looking him over again. Damn, he was hot!

He looked at me, fear in his eyes. "I mean, where *are* we?" "Oh, that's what I'm trying to figure out," I said, shrugging my shoulders. "Oh," he said. "Do you know what just happened to me? All I can remember is the hospital bed, and then these guys in black came into my room and shot me with something, and then . . . nothing," he said, his voice falling at the end of his story.

Suddenly, I was hit with a pang of unease. I didn't want to be the one to tell him that he wasn't exactly human anymore. That he would see multiple physical changes and experience things that didn't count as puberty. That he now had bat-like wings, a scaly torso, and retractable claws on his hands and feet. It was hard enough that I had to be told by the workers that I was no longer the same person I once was and I didn't want this boy to suffer the same.

"Well, it's a long, painful story. I'll tell you about it later," I said, chickening out. He was bound to find out anyway. "No, tell me now," he insisted, his eyes prodding mine. I shifted uneasily. "Well, umm, try to feel your hair," I said awkwardly. He looked at me warily, as if I was playing some kind of game. "I'm not screwing with you," I added. He did not take his eyes off of me as he placed his hands on his head and moved them around. He looked doubtful until his hands felt the two sharp bumps on either side of his head.

"What happened to my head?" he asked me, acting as if they were just bumps he got, no more than an accident on the playground. "Those are horns." "Horns?" he asked, not believing anything I said. I sighed. "If you don't believe me, then take off your shirt," I said, then blushed. Had I seriously asked a guy to take off his shirt?

He looked at me like I was crazy. "Uh, absolutely not!" he said, backing away from me and standing up. "You don't have to take it all off," I said, averting my eyes, "just look at your navel. You'll see a difference." He looked like he wanted to get as far away from me as possible. "I don't believe you," he said. I looked at him to insist, but I saw him blushing. "Why are you so embarrassed?" I asked him. "I'll show you mine if you show me yours," he said, not looking at me, his face a deep crimson. I shrugged. "Okay," I said, and lifted my black shirt until we could see my entire stomach. He looked at it and gasped. "Your skin . . . what happened to it?" he asked in shock. I looked at my dark, olive green scales and thought, *is his green, too*?

"My skin isn't like yours," he said unconvincingly, his hands poised on the ends of his shirt. "I have normal skin." "Just take a little peek. It can't hurt," I said. He closed his eyes and took a deep breath. Then he lifted up his shirt. He looked at his skin with terrified eyes as his midnight blue scales gleamed softly in the dim light. "No," he cried, and fell to his feet in sobs. He knew his life would never be the same. I felt sorry for Severin. It was hard when I learned that I could never have a family, the mate of my choice, normal children, and a normal life. I could feel his pain.

I gave him time to wallow in his misery alone while I explored our new compound. There was a small daybed with a roll out underneath, one bathroom, an empty closet that reeked of mothballs, a chest with old dusty books and board games, and I guess the room Severin was in was the living room. I was in the bedroom, wondering why this compound was built in the first place, when the door that lead to the outside swung open with a violent force, shaking the walls.

"Come out here! You can't hide anymore!" said an angry masculine voice. I jumped with a start. It wasn't Aaron, and I've never heard the workers sound like that. With a scary realization, I found that I was frozen in place in fear. Severin yelped loudly from the living room, startling me into motion. Adrenaline rushed through my blood stream as I practically flew down the stinking hallway to the living room. Severin was in the headlock of a heavy set man, struggling to get free.

"Let go of him!" I cried angrily. I recalled the training I had taken these past five weeks of life and jumped on the man's back. I let loose my claws on his shoulders as they sliced into his flesh and hit bone, blood gushing out of the wound as I scratched the bone and peeled back his flesh. He howled in pain and released Severin right before I dragged my bloody claws from his shoulders to his throat. "Jenny, send backup!" the man screamed. The outburst surprised me just long enough for the man to get free of my grasp. "Don't fight with me. You're coming with me," he said, his blue eyes enraged. He took out a gun and pointed it at me. Fast as lightening, I jumped out of the way when he pulled the trigger. There was no sound, and they weren't bullets he was shooting.

Of course. They were sleeping darts.

He shot again, and I barely made it out of the way as the dart whizzed past my face. My heart pounded in my chest. This was going to be difficult. Suddenly, the door opened to reveal three people dressed in black, one woman, two men. The men came up from behind me and tried to grab my arms. I jerked away and ran towards the bathroom.

Unfortunately, the woman caught up with me as soon as I touched the door. She grabbed my arms and ran me into the wall head first. I struggled to get away, but the woman now had the two men to help her hold me in place. Out of the corner of my eye, I saw the heavy man come up behind me with a hypodermic needle filled with a neon green liquid.

Oh no.

He put the sharp needle on my arm and was about to inject me with that liquid when something I never thought would happen happened.

Severin, looking weak, was attempting to run to me. "No! Severin, this isn't your fight!" I cried. He was a newbie—he couldn't possibly win this battle. One of the men holding me released me and easily caught Severin. "Okay, this is *too* easy," the woman said. The heavy man stuck the needle into my arm and squeezed. "Well, the girl sure isn't," the man said, and laughed.

I started to feel weak the second the liquid hit my bloodstream. My blood circulated slowly through my veins and my eyelids felt like lead when I blinked. I couldn't lift my arms, much less kick my legs. "Did she cause those cuts?" one of the men asked. "Yeah. She's obviously had some kick ass training," he said, touching the bone-deep cuts on his right arm gently.

"Perfect. That's just what we need," said one of the men. *Why can't I fight?* I asked myself mentally, struggling to give the woman a good punch, to no avail. The humans holding me released me, letting me fall to the floor in a crumpled heap. I was surprised that I had the strength to cushion my fall with my arms at the last moment. I heard a loud thump next to me, and next thing I knew, Severin was laying next to me. The humans left, leaving me and Severin alone in the hallway.

"What's going to happen to us?" Severin asked weakly, not of fear, but of the toxins that they gave us. "I don't know," I said, my voice much more feeble than Severin's. It was appropriate; my throat felt like it's been sanded down for hours and left a dry, aching feeling in its wake. "The lab is a high security place. This had never happened before."

The four humans came back, each holding a pair of handcuffs. The man that I had cut was now wearing a bandage on his shoulders, along with a clean white shirt.

"Alright, let's tie them up," he said, bending down and clasping one of the handcuffs to my ankles. My fear was easily replaced by fury, and I tried to move my foot. I was only able to move it about and inch and my efforts were rewarded with a slap to the face. "Don't do this, sweetie. The more you move, the more the anti virus takes effect." He was right. I was already beginning to feel even weaker.

"Where are you taking us?" asked Severin, the locks already placed on his hands and feet. "To a place where you can be normal again," the woman said, then laughed. The man helping the woman picked Severin up and began to walk out the door. The other man picked me up with a surprising gentleness and followed the others.

Once out the door, I looked to the left and saw the crate that I had lived in for the five weeks of my new life, and felt a pang of sadness that I might never see it again, even though I hated it. The anti virus circulating through my body was making me weaker and sleepier by the second. The gentle rocking of my captor's arms made me feel like a baby being rocked to sleep.

The humans went through the door and into the long white hallway. We passed the training room, where I learned how to fight; the testing labs, where I first breathed life as a freak mutant; the kitchen, where they made the slop that tasted disgusting.

Finally, we made it to the door. It was bashed in severely, as if the humans had used a crowbar and, knowing the lab's security, a few sticks of dynamite. I could tell because of the black explosion marks all around the place where the door used to fit perfectly. The man carried me outside, where I met a beautiful sight: little white stars in a black sky. They shimmered like diamonds in black velvet, and filled me with a peace and serenity I hadn't felt before. All this occurred from looking at the night sky.

My captors carried me to a large white van. They popped open the large trunk and placed me and Severin inside it. "You two might as well sleep. We have a long drive ahead of us," the woman said. "Now don't you two do anything dirty," the scratched man said with a naughty grin as he closed the trunk door. I sighed and laid against the soft, thick carpeting, exhausted. Severin was on the opposite side of me, his eyes drooping. All of a sudden, there was an earth rattling *boom!* That shook the entire van. Bright light

14

seeped into the cracks of the van next to the van. "What was that? What's going to happen to us?" he asked softly. "I don't know, Severin," I said, a little shaken by the sudden loud noise. "I don't know."

Chapter Three

The van bumped to what had to be the thousandth stop that night. We had been driving for six hours, and a soft, violet glow was beginning to streak across the sky. Severin was curled up against my body, sleeping as if he was dead. His midnight black hair was under my chin and his face was pressed against my neck. At first I wanted to push him away, but then I remembered that this was his first day of life as a freak mutant. Besides, he was just too adorable in sleep to wake.

I had tried to get some sleep, but the constant motion of the van kept me awake until I gave up trying. Severin stirred besides me and opened his eyes. "Had a good rest?" I asked him. "Whoa, sorry," he said, embarrassed by the way he slept and moved out of his position. "It's okay," I said, and gave him a once-over. The weakening effects of the anti virus seemed to have disappeared on both me and him completely, though he was wide awake and I was sluggishly sleepy. "You look tired," he said, a frown deepening his handsome face. "You need to sleep." "I couldn't. Not with the car moving like this, anyway," I said.

"Here," he said, and moved his handcuffed arms around my body. His strong arms encased me as I was pressed against his solid, warm body. God, it felt good. I didn't realize how cold I was until he pulled me closer and I buried my head into his chest. It was then that I noticed how perfectly well my body fit into his. It was a perfect match—we fit together nicely.

I was just about to drift off when the van suddenly shut off. Geez, were we finally there? The trunk door popped open to reveal the heavy man staring down at us.

"We are at a gas station. If you need to use the bathroom, then come with me now." I looked at Severin. "No, I'm fine," I said. "Me too," Severin agreed. "Okay," he said, "I'm closing the trunk, but don't you two dare to even think of escape. I'll be right here," he said, and slowly closed the trunk. A few minutes later, the car started rolling again. "You know," Severin said, "I never asked for your name." "It's Violet," I replied sleepily, nestling my face deeper into his chest. "We need to think of a way to get out of here," he said pointedly. I thought of all the training I learned in my first week of life about what to do if I had gotten kidnapped. Always carry a weapon. Never let them grab you. They told me that if I acted like a helpless girl, then the benefit of doubt would work in my favor. Unfortunately, Severin was a male. Besides, we were both freak mutants.

I guess now was the time to act like one.

"I have a plan," said with a tired smile and touched my black socks.

*   *   *

Three hours later, the vehicle reached its final destination. That's what their GPS said, at least.

"Ready?" I asked Severin. He nodded. I remembered that I had a knife hidden in my sock, and had been able to saw away the handcuffs successfully, even though it took a while. Severin and I lay together to pretend we were still trapped when the trunk door opened, bathing us in a bright orange glow. "Come on," I heard the woman say, and was grabbed roughly by the arm. One of the men grabbed Severin and hauled him out of the trunk.

"Wait a minute," the woman said, looking in the trunk and finding the broken handcuff chains. "Now!" I yelled at Severin, pulling my arm free and giving the woman a good punch in the face. She fell to the ground, seemingly unconscious.

Severin gave a pretty good smack to the guy holding him, but it wasn't enough to knock him down. "Hit him in the temple!" I said to Severin, turning to the other man.

I saw a needle with the green liquid in his right hand and a dart gun in his left. *Not this time brother* I thought, and lunged at him. My hands closed around his neck as he fell to the ground. I kicked the gun away when he tried to use it as a lever to get me off. I grabbed his right hand as it tried to shoot me with the anti virus. I used my mouth and bit the neon green liquid away from him and spat it away.

Then the man really began to struggle. My hand pressed down into his throat until his lips turned blue and his struggling stopped. I hopped off of him to see Severin crouching over the man that attacked him. "Impressive," I said. He smiled.

The heavy set man was nowhere to be seen, so we made ourselves scarce. We were surrounded by trees with only a tall white building and a long winding road to show civilization. We ran in the direction we came in, with only the patting of our feet and our labored breaths filling the silence. Just when my vision began to get blurry from the exercise, we met up with a closed up fence.

"Should we climb it?" asked Severin breathlessly, his face red with exhaustion. I heard a faint buzzing sound coming from the fence. That could mean only one thing.

"No, it's an electric fence," I said. I looked right and left, trying to find another way out. There wasn't; the fence seemed to wrap around the entire building. I refused to let despair cloud my judgment. I looked at Severin. "Close your eyes and turn away," I told him firmly. "Okay . . ." he said, closing his eyes and turning away. When I was sure he wasn't looking, I quickly took off my shirt and spread out my wings. I let them stretch for a moment, enjoying their strength.

Then I began to flap.

I didn't know how to fly, but I was going to try it with all my might. I flapped my wings hard, but with no result. I tried jumping, only to hover for a moment and then land flat on my face into the soft brown earth.

"Are you okay back there, Violet?" Severin asked, his back still turned. "Yeah," I said through gritted teeth. I tried once more, only to end up with the same results. I sighed, giving up. My face was filthy, and my body just the same. Scratches littered my stomach, making little designs and giving a raw feeling to my skin. I quickly grabbed my tee and turned around.

"It's okay to look now, Severin," I said. He turned around. "What happened to your face?" he asked, coming up close to me. "I was trying to fly," I responded, wiping my face with the back of my hand. He looked uncertain. "You have wings?" he asked. "Yes, and you do too," I said. "They are under an invisible patch of skin on your back." He sighed. "I guess I shouldn't be surprised, since you're just like me," he said, his head hanging down.

"Hey, it's nothing to be ashamed of. It's really kind of cool," I said, putting my hand on his shoulder. "But how do we get out of here?" he asked me, his soulful blue eyes boring into mine. I was speechless for a moment, drowning in those eyes. *Snap out of it!* I kicked myself mentally.

I was thinking of a way to respond when I was interrupted by a strange cawing noise. I looked up to see a large bird of prey in a tree, looking at me. It flew down from the tree and landed a mere five feet from me and Severin. Its amber eyes stared intensely into mine.

"Violet, what's wrong?" Severin asked, and then looked at the bird. I was pretty sure it was a falcon. It looked at us a while longer, then took a running start, spread its wings, and glided to the tree. "Maybe I should try it that way," I said absently. "Try what?" Severin asked. "Wait, what are you doing?!" he said, startled as I whipped off my shirt in front of him and spread my wings. He backed away as I ran away from the fence. I stopped for a few moments. Then I took off in full speed towards the fence. When the timing seemed right, I kicked out my wings and jumped.

This time I soared over the fence, the wind rippling through my hair and pushing against my face. My wings had never felt so powerful as it carried me away from Severin and over the fence. I instinctively leaned my body downward after I crossed the fence and put my feet in front of me. But instead of the soft landing I was hoping for, I fell flat on my face. Again.

"Severin!" I cried breathlessly, "do what I just did! It was so cool!" He looked unsure, but backed away from the fence. He started to run, but stopped when he needed to spread his wings. "I can't," he said, looking frightened. "It might help if you took your shirt off," I said, then immediately felt my cheeks catch fire. He looked at me weirdly. "Well, unless you want to rip your clothes, then I would suggest you take it off," I said, feeling my face redden like a tomato. He sighed and took his shirt clean off.

I tried hard not to ogle at his bare torso. He experimentally spread his dark blue wings to their full length. "They don't even feel heavy," he said in wonder. I was surprised I could keep from smiling. He took off running, spread his wings, and jumped.

He soared over the fence, the wind making his black hair ruffle in the wind. I began to feel weak in the knees by his godly beauty. Unfortunately, he had the same landing as me. "You made it," I said, ruffling his windblown hair. It was like silk beneath my fingers. "Maybe we can fly away home now," he said, just as exhilarated as me.

"Sounds great, but first, we need to find out where we are," I said.

I heard a familiar cawing from behind me. I turned to see the falcon staring back at us. "Thank you," I whispered.

I don't know if the bird understood my gratitude, but it seemed to nod slightly before flying away.

"Come on," Severin said excitedly behind me. "Let's fly."

I squared my shoulders and took off running at full speed. I allowed my wings to spread full length before jumping off into the air. The thin layer of membranes that spread across my wing bones and allowed me to fly lifted and caught as air carried me farther away from the building. Severin wasn't far behind me as we both soared north on our way to freedom.

I looked back to catch a glimpse at the fence. It looked like any other fence, only with something small and white attached to the top of the door. I looked closer.

It was a security camera.

Chapter Four

Hours passed, but Severin and I kept meeting up with more trees and forest. Even though gliding made us go a lot faster, we always ended up meeting up with the ground, forcing us to run and jump every few minutes. By the time we reached a sign that said "Welcome to Wisconsin", we were exhausted.

"Well, I guess we should take the next exit and look for food," said Severin, his voice barely a whisper from all the exercise. "We should," I responded, "but let's rest for a minute."

We saw a giant tree that looked critter free, and decided to get some shut eye for a while. We collapsed under the tree's shade in an exhausted heap. We sat propped up against the tree trunk, my head on his shoulder. It was then that I remembered that we were both half-naked.

"Um, I should probably put my shirt back on," I said sheepishly, getting up. "No, it's okay," Severin said, pulling me down next to him. He put his arm around my shoulders and pulled me close. "It's a little cold out here," he said, shivering. "Do we have any powers against that?" I thought for a moment. "I don't think so," I said. "If we do, then we wouldn't be feeling the cold."

"Oh," he said. We sat in silence for a while, our limbs relaxing. Then he asked something that threw me completely off guard. "Why were we created in the first place?" he asked softly, his hand stroking my long, uncontrollable wavy brown hair.

"Hmm," I said, leaning into his warmth, thinking. "I think it's because of something that will kill the humans. We have to protect them or something," I finally answered. He was silent for a moment. "But if they treat us the way the lab workers treated us, what makes them think we will protect them?" he asked, his hand now stroking up and down my arm, sending small shivers of pleasure throughout my body.

"Uh," I said, putting my cold hand over his wandering fingers. "I don't know," I said, as he leaned over me. "Am I making you uncomfortable?" he asked quietly, his eyes seeking mine. I looked away. "A little," I answered, shrugging out of his grasp. I stood up and he grabbed my hand. "Is it a coincidence that they created a male and female mutant?" he asked. "Yes," I answered slowly, knowing where this conversation was going. "We should be on our way now."

"But . . ." he started. "No more talk of this," I said harshly, grabbing his hand and pulling him up. He looked as if he wanted to say something, but shut up when I made a running start and spread my wings. I jumped higher than usual and soared up over the trees, wind hissing through my hair.

I looked at the clouds, which seemed to get darker and darker the higher I went up. A loud rumbling rippled through the sky, and a sudden light struck the ground right in front of me! I tried to jerk to a halt, but ended up falling in a death spiral to the earth. I screamed, losing control of myself, trying to flap in the rough air. The ground rushed up to meet me at nauseating speed, my head facing downward. I knew I wouldn't be able to make it. I closed my eyes as I prepared for impact.

But I didn't land the way I had anticipated. Instead, arms surrounded my body around my waist, sheer milliseconds before my head would have been scrambled eggs on the asphalt.

"Are you okay?" asked a distressed Severin. "Are you hurt?" "I'm okay," I said, my body completely upside down. "Can you put me down right side up?" He positioned his hands, and within moments, I was on my feet. "Thanks," I said gratefully, not meeting his eyes. "No problem," he said, wrapping me quick hug. "What was that?" he asked.

"I think the light was lightening," I replied. "And the noise was thunder. A storm is brewing."

As if to respond, rain began to pour down, soaking us instantly. "Come on, we need to find someplace dry," he said, grabbing my hand and pulling me along with him. I guess we both decided to put off flying for a while.

At first, the rain was a small downpour, but it got more and more severe the further we went. Severin and I put our shirts back on to conserve our body heat in the now dropping temperature, as well as the rain getting so loud that we could barely hear our own thoughts.

"How much further do you think the forest is?" Severin practically yelled next to me. "I don't know!" I yelled back. "But we have to keep moving!"

It seemed like forever, but we finally made it out of the forest, and the road split into two paths. One kept on going, while the other lead to some buildings that looked promising. "This way," I said to Severin, pulling him to the road that leads to a bunch of buildings. There was one that smelled wonderful and had a sign that said "McDonalds" on the bottom of a yellow "m". "Let's go in there," I said, and pulled him inside.

The inside of "McDonalds" smelled better than the outside. The inside was comforting, and, best of all, it was warm and dry, with food. "Can we eat something?" Severin asked. "No, we need this thing called 'money'. I don't really know what it looks like." Severin, stared at the menu board hungrily. "We can't eat anything," I said, "but we can stay here until the rain stops."

He led me to a table with a soft padding on the back of the chair. We were both shivering violently, our teeth chattering. "Come here," Severin said, opening his arms to me. I gladly accepted the invitation and wrapped my arms around him. Despite the wetness of his shirt, he was very warm. Sighing, I leaned into his warmth. He buried his face in my hair.

"Hey, you kids got any money?" a woman's voice asked, tearing us apart. "No," I answered, my voice raw. The woman standing in front of me was short with blonde hair and green eyes. She was dressed in a denim jacket with blue jeans and a green shirt. "Let me buy something for you," she said, unzipping what had to be her purse. "You two look miserable. And what's with the dirty face? Are you two homeless?" Severin nodded, not really knowing what she meant, but accepting the fact that she was going to buy us some food. I, on the other hand, started to feel a little strange. "Okay, well, I know a place where you can spend the night. There's going to be a lot of rain tonight. By the way, my name is Cindy," she said. "I'll go buy your food. Stay where you are," she said, and hurried off to the counter. Severin turned to me.

"Well, that was easy," he said, and cracked a grin. I grinned back uncertainty, my warning instincts kicking in. I learned in the training center to never trust humans that appeared nice to you. If they came on too strong, then they might have darker intentions underneath the sugar coated surface.

"Severin, I don't think we can trust her," I said urgently to him. "What do you mean? She seems nice," he said, confused by my words. "We'll just take the food, and tell her that we do have a place to stay," I said. Severin looked at me like I was crazy. "She said it was going to rain all night," he said. "Let's stay where she wants us to, and we'll be dry. What's there to worry about?" I opened my mouth to respond when Cindy came back with food in her hands.

"Eat up. You two can stay at my house for as long as you want. I'll take good care of you," she said, smiling sweetly. "Uh, thanks, but we'll be fine. We don't need to stay at your place," I said. "Oh, nonsense," she replied. "You two will catch your death in this type of weather."

I accepted the food in my hands, defeated. It wasn't only about me now, but Severin as well. If I survived, he survived. He wasn't more than two days old, and it was my responsibility to take care of him until he could go off on his own. "Okay," I said, not meeting the woman's eyes. I couldn't shake the feeling that something was wrong. It went deeper than uncertainty. It was like Cindy had some type of evil vibes coming from her. It was scary and not at all natural.

She leaned towards Severin, a chill racing down my spine. I did *not* want her close to him. "That's right," she said softly. "I'll take care of you." Did I imagine it, or did her eyes really just change color from green to yellow? "Severin," I said warningly, standing up, my strange feelings morphing into fear. "What is it, dear?" she asked me, her yellow eyes probing me. "Do you not like the burger?" Her voice was suddenly deeper, not at all like the sweet voice earlier. "Violet," the woman said, and with a shock I realized her hands now had claws. I jumped away from the table. "How do you know my name?" I asked her. "What are you?"

"I am the hunter," she said, and laughed a not entirely sane laugh. "I am the one who came to kill you. I am shadow, I am light. I am life, I am death. I am the one who kills creatures like you," she said wickedly, and lunged towards me.

Her ugly claws closed in around my throat, cutting off my air supply. "Severin! Help me!" I choked out. He seemed frozen for a moment, then jumped on top of the woman-creature's back. He let loose his claws, piercing the creature's throat and shoulders. "Ahh!" she screamed out. She released me as I fell to the floor. She bucked, making Severin fly off of her and hit the wall, landing on his stomach on the floor. She turned on him.

"Bitch!" she snarled. "I can kill you first. You first, then the girl," she said, and jumped on his back. "Severin!" I cried, and jumped on top of her. I retracted my claws and pushed them through her rough skin as far as it could go, until it went all the way through her neck. Before Cindy could tell what I was doing, I sliced her head off, bone and everything. Instead of dark red blood, there was a yellowish powder covering my claws.

And man did it stink!

The creature's head rolled off of her body, coming to a stop at the near wall. Severin's eyes were wide with panic, and his breath was labored. The smell of sulfur and brimstone coated the air as a yellow dust emitted from the dead body.

"Let's get out of here," Severin said weakly, grabbing my hand. I didn't resist. We ran out of the building and into the rain. It wasn't as harsh this time, but it was still very cold, and the rain kept coming down. "Come on," I said. "We need to find a place to stay."

We had walked around for a while, looking for a dry place to spend the now approaching night. The rain had let up until it was a mere drizzle, allowing us the advantage of the sidewalk. We walked for hours until we found a place. It was a small hole dug up by some animal behind a dumpster, the roof of the dumpster shielding the hole from the rain.

"We can stay here," I said, leading Severin to our new temporary home. It was too small to fit the both of us, so we dug it out until we were practically underneath the dumpster. It was more of a burrow now. There was a wall close to the dumpster, so we didn't have much space. Luckily, there was an exhaust heater next to the wall blowing into the hole, so I knew we would be warm that night.

"Is this really more comfortable than at the labs?" Severin asked as we lay together in the cramped burrow. "Yes," I answered. "In the labs, they kept me in a dog crate. No bed, blankets, pillows. Nothing. This is actually very comfortable," I added, patting the brown earth. "But it sure doesn't smell right," he said, and chuckled. "Yeah, a giant trashcan wasn't one of my top choices either," I said, and chuckled along with him.

Strangely, I didn't mind the smell as long as Severin's arms were around me. My face pressed into his chest, inhaling his scent. He smelled wonderful, like mountain air. We were quiet for a moment. Then Severin said, "You got upset when I asked you if it was a coincidence that they created a male and female mutant. Why?" I didn't want to answer, but did anyway. "Because it wasn't a coincidence," I said softly. "They wanted us to . . . mate. They didn't want to spend more money making us, so they created you to uh . . . breed with me," I said in a rush.

Severin was quiet for a moment, processing this new information. Then his arms pulled at me tighter. "Would you have done so, if we hadn't been kidnapped?" he asked me softly into my hair. "I swear, you're just like a toddler," I said instead, desperately trying to turn the conversation somewhere else. "You are always asking questions."

"That didn't answer my question," he said, and I slumped, my plan not really working. I thought for a moment, thinking of a way to explain my feelings. "Maybe," was all I came up with. He seemed satisfied with that answer though, so I didn't say anything afterward. "Let's go to sleep."

We were awakened the next morning by the sound of human voices. "Did you hear about that laboratory in Canada? It was totally robbed!" came a female voice. "Yeah. I heard they made some kind of experiment with teens there," said a male voice. Severin looked at me, and knowledge passed between us. "That was *our* lab," he whispered. "Shh," I murmured, listening closely.

"All of the workers were found dead, but they couldn't find the teens. They did find the blueprints of them, though. I think there are two of them," said the female. "Yeah, one boy and one girl. The girl was created first, though, so she should be one tough cookie," said the male. There was a large *bang* on top of us, making Severin and me jump.

"What do you think happened to the teens? I hope they're okay," said the female. "The robbers probably took them. But knowing what those workers did to the girl, she is probably able to fend for herself. The boy, on the other hand . . ." the voices faded as they went inside the building.

Severin and I looked at each other wide eyed. "Everyone died?" Severin asked quietly. "I hope not," I said, shocked. I secretly hoped Aaron was okay. Even though he was a pain in my ass, he was still kind of like a father to me. If anything had happened to him, someone was going to get hurt.

"We need to go," Severin said, and crawled out of our little stinky hole. He took my hand and helped me out. "We need to get back to the lab," I said. "But I don't know where we are."

"Maybe we should ask around," Severin said, rubbing his hands up and down my arms in an attempt to keep me warm. "Well, I did see a sign that said 'Wisconsin', so I guess we are in the United States. I'm not sure how far, though," I said. I grabbed Severin's right hand and began to lead him away from the dumpster. We walked around, hand in hand, looking for any indication that we were heading the right way. We didn't see anything—just an endless plane of trees and fast food restaurants.

"You've never eaten anything as a mutant yet," I said suddenly as we walked past another restaurant. "I guess not," Severin said as his stomach rumbled for the third time. I looked at him and saw, for the first time, how much paler he looked and weaker he was from yesterday. "You need to eat something," I said. "You really don't look too good." "What is there to eat that doesn't require money?" he asked me. I sighed and looked down. It was hopeless. Then I looked at the dumpster near the restaurant wall. Someone was taking out the trash. The trash bag ripped, spilling out food contents that seemed edible.

Maybe not I thought, and smiled.

Chapter Five

"I can't believe we just ate out of the dump," Severin said, his arm around my shoulders as we sat on the bench, enjoying the sunny-yet-cold day just a little better.

We had made sure nobody was watching before we jumped into the dumpster and ate our fill. The trash was fresh, and we were careful to eat around the bite marks that the customers had made. There was even soda and water bottles that were half full.

When we were finished, Severin and I had walked around until several children ran past us, racing to a nearby playground around a few roads leading to lots of houses. There was a bench next to it, so we decided to rest.

"I'll bet your breath smells delicious," I said, bumping my shoulder against his. "Yours too, so don't even think about breathing on me," he said, tightening his arm around me. I smiled and closed my eyes, leaning into his warmth.

"Violet?" he asked softly. "Yes?" I said. "Do you remember anything about your human family?" he asked. I didn't answer; I found out a long time ago that it was better not to think about it. I opened my eyes to look at him, but was rewarded by his face mere inches from mine. "I'd rather not talk about it," I said, trying to look away but failing miserably. I didn't move, didn't want to. His face loomed ever closer, his eyes like pools of soft, blue water. I felt myself drowning in those endlessly deep pools. His eyes asked, *is this okay?* I don't know what my answer was, but it must have said yes, because a second later, his lips touched mine with the warm softness of a butterfly's wings.

His arms wrapped around my waist, pulling me closer as the kiss deepened. Somehow, my arms found their way to his shoulders, snaking around his neck. I knew this was wrong, knew I should stop the kiss.

My body didn't listen. Actually, stopping was the last thing I wanted to do. I tried to pull him closer, but we were already so tightly pressed, yet I tried. Believe me, I tried.

"Hey, get a room!" someone said right next to us. Severin and I jumped apart, looking in embarrassment at the boy who interrupted us. He seemed about seventeen, and he was very good looking. He had brown hair, hazel eyes, and tanned skin. "You guys must not be from around here," he said. "You visiting or something?" "Uh, yeah," I said, trying to fight the embarrassing blush creeping to my cheeks. "Really?" the boy said. "Then where are you from? How long will you be staying?"

"Um, we are from Canada, and I don't know how long we will be staying," Severin said, putting a protective arm around me, which I shrugged off. I wasn't sure what the whole kissing thing meant to him, and I wasn't ready for more physical contact with him just yet. "Canada? Wasn't there a robbery in a lab there?" he asked, plopping himself besides me. "I guess," I said, scooting away from him and accidentally ended up cuddling with Severin. This guy didn't have the same vibes as that demonic woman, but that didn't make him the easiest person to talk to.

"Say, you guys play basketball up there? I was on the way to meet my buddy, Steve, for a rematch. You can come and watch," he said. I looked at Severin. "It can't hurt," he said. I thought for a moment. "Okay, just for a little while," I said, getting up. "Great. We're right over there," he said, and began walking towards a bunch of trees and houses with a small road to lead the way.

"By the way," the boy said as Severin got up to follow. "My name is Aaron."

Chapter Six

I almost completely stopped in my tracks. Of all the names in the world, did his name just *have* to be Aaron? Sensing my distress, Severin grabbed my hand. "Are you okay?" he asked. "Is he a demon like that woman?" "No," I whispered. "His name is Aaron."

"Hey, what's the holdup?" Aaron asked, at least fifty yards away. "Just chatting," Severin said smoothly, dragging me along with him as he walked. "The basketball court is just around the corner. Do you guys know how to play? I can teach you if you don't," he said as we stepped in place besides him.

Aaron was a very talkative boy, and, by the way he kept twitching, it looked like he had some kind of hyperactive disorder. But that was okay; the real Aaron was the complete opposite, which gave me some comfort.

"How were you two able to come here together if you're dating? Didn't your parents give you any trouble?" Aaron asked. Severin and I were silent for a moment, not sure how to answer. "Um, I guess you can say that we ran away together," I said carefully. I tried not to accidentally slip on a word; that would leave him suspicious. "Oh," he said. "How long have you two been together? I can only stay interested in a girl for about two weeks," he said. I looked at Severin for some help. "Uh, not too long," he said. "About a week, maybe."

Aaron stopped, a confused look in his gaze. "But if you've only been together a week, then why did you run off so soon?" he asked. I sent a glare of daggers to Severin for getting us into this mess. "Our parents wanted us to do things we weren't comfortable with," I said after a minute of thinking. Aaron lifted an eyebrow. "What kinds of things? Things that are illegal?"

"Yes," I said, playing along. "Do you guys have a place to stay? There's an old abandoned house three blocks from my house. It's a little hazardous, but Steve and I hang out over there at night every now and then. It's believed to be haunted, but Steve and I had out there enough to know that they are just rumors. There are separate rooms if you still don't feel safe with, well, you know . . ."

"Yes, we get it," said before he could say any more. "And thanks for the offer. I think we'll take it. We haven't had a decent place to stay for quite some time," I said. "Okay," Aaron said. Aaron babbled on and on as we passed lots of houses. A neighborhood, I think it is called. I listened on and off as Aaron chattered away at how to play basketball. It really didn't seem very interesting, but a sneaky peek at Severin told me otherwise. He seemed to be hanging on to every word that came out of Aaron's mouth.

A few minutes later, we turned on a corner and arrived at a fenced-in place covered in concrete with two poles with baskets attached. Four boys sat on a bench with towels on their necks. They talked to each other, neither one of them noticing our arrival.

"Hey, Steve!" Aaron said, waving at one of the boys. One of the boys looked up. I froze when the beautiful boy revealed his face. He had hair the color of gold, eyes as green as the leaves of trees and the depth of a deep ocean. His skin was deeply bronzed, and muscles rippled across his arms and legs as he got up and walked towards us. My eyes roamed across his handsome body, checking him out from head to toe.

"Hey, Aaron. I thought you weren't going to show up," he said. Steve looked towards me and Severin. We locked eyes as time literally seemed to slow. I completely forgot about Severin's hand that held mine. All I could feel was the heat in Steve's gaze as we looked each other over. "I see you brought some new friends," Steve said, breaking eye contact between us. I looked down quickly, fighting the fiery heat creeping up my neck to my cheeks.

What the hell was that all about? I just kissed Severin, and now I already want to cheat on him? I squeezed Severin's hand and backed into his familiar warmth.

"Yeah," Aaron said. "They are runaways from Canada. They are going to stay in the old Jankinson house for the night. Did you ever know that they don't know how to play basketball?" Aaron chatted away. "Okay then," Steve interrupted. "Let's see if we can teach them before it gets dark. What are their names, anyway?" "Uh," Aaron said, turning to us. "I'm Severin, and this is Violet," Severin said. "Nice to meet you two," Steve said, shaking our hands. Steve's hands were warm as they touched mine. A hot tingle shot up my arm as a shiver of pleasure made its way up my spine. He must've felt it too, because he dropped my hand much quicker than Severin's. "Come on," he said. "Let's see how well you play."

Chapter Seven

Basketball didn't turn out to be very fun for me. After a few tries, I was almost literally drenched in sweat, despite the cold temperature. Though I hate to admit it, training back in the lab was much easier than this torture.

"I think I'll sit down now," I said. "Are you sure?" Severin asked, concern masking his exhilaration of playing. "Yes," I answered reassuringly. "Go have fun."

He took my advice to heart.

The three boys on the bench stared at me strangely; as if they were looking right through me. It was enough to give me the creeps, but their vibes didn't seem as demonic as Cindy's. They stared at me a moment longer, then left. I wasn't sure what the whole thing was about them, but I decided to ignore it.

Not long after I sat down to catch my breath had Steve sat down right next to me. "Severin seems to be having fun," he noted. He caught me completely off guard, so I looked at him dumbly for a moment before I understood what he said.

"Yeah, I guess he must like basketball," I said, struggling not to look at his face. His nearness crept into me, making me nervous. "Are you two lost or something?" he asked. I wasn't sure how to answer honestly; he would think I was crazy. "Yes, but I don't think we would want to be found yet," I said, thinking about what would happen if any of the workers found us. And let me tell you, I sure as heck didn't want to go back to the lab.

"Why did you run away?" Steve asked, obviously satisfied with my answer. "Um, our parents wanted us to do some stuff we didn't feel ready for," I said, giving him the same answer as Aaron. "Wait, do you mean . . ." Steve said, his eyes growing wide. "Yes," I answered quickly. "I don't really like to talk about it." "Okay," he said, and sat silent, thinking to himself.

"Are you two, like, together?" he asked suddenly, taking me by surprise. "Yes," I said, and wanted to kick myself.

"Really," he said. "He doesn't seem your type." I looked at him. Big mistake. His eyes drowned me, making me feel like I was being splashed with hot water. "And you feel like you are?" I retorted sharply, my voice surprisingly steady. "Maybe," he said, and smiled. Oh my god, that smile was so godly. He looked like an angel, only missing his halo and wings . . . .

Right when I thought about wings, my own started to tug at my back eagerly. Pain shot up around my back as I struggled to keep them concealed. *Why is this happening* I thought, beginning to panic. *This never happened before.*

"Hey, are you okay?" Steve asked, leaning towards me. My wings pulled harder, desperate to burst free. It strained at my back until I was sure the skin would break!

"I just need some air," I gasped. Steve immediately leaned back. "Do I need to get Severin?" he asked, getting up and turning away. "No," I said. "I'll be fine. Really," I said, though it did little to reassure him. "Okay," he said, and walked away to finish the game. My wings no longer wanted to come out right when Steve left my side. *What was that all about* I asked myself. Unfortunately, there was no one to answer.

*   *   *

"So this will be your stop for the night," Aaron said as we stepped inside the old building. The floorboards creaked under our weight as the house swayed from a strong breeze from outside. The house was only lit from the dim light of candles that Aaron had so thoughtfully brought.

"Steve and I will get what you will need for the night. We will eat here with you guys and stay until you feel safe. We have school tomorrow, so we can't stay long," Aaron said. "Steve is ordering pizza for us tonight. I hope you like cheese. Then again, I can't think of anyone who wouldn't like cheese . . ."

Aaron kept babbling, so I had tuned him out. The house smelled like mold and looked like crap. It was a one story building with two bedrooms, one bathroom (which didn't work anyway), a kitchen, and a storage room. Severin was looking around, seemingly interested in his new surroundings. That, or he was just tired of hearing Aaron talk. Aaron was just about to tell me about his favorite baseball team when Steve came in to save the day with pizza in hand.

"I see Aaron is talking again," he said. "I'll get the duck tape." "No, you don't need to do that again," Aaron said quickly. "I'll shut up." "Good boy." "What do you mean 'again'," I asked curiously. These two had a weird dynamic; Steve was calm while Aaron was hyper, and talkative where Steve was quiet. They did seem to make good buddies, though.

Aaron laughed at my question. "Boy, there's a story to tell! There was this one time in a beta meeting at school where I kept talking . . ."

"Uh, let me tell the story," Steve said. "You don't add enough details." He turned to me. "It all started that morning as we were walking to school. Aaron saw this girl that he really liked-," "No I didn't!" Aaron interrupted. "You barely stopped looking at her in that beta meeting," Steve said to him, then focused his attention on me again.

"Aaron kept trying to get her attention, but he ended up annoying everyone else. But luckily for us, I had brought a roll of duck tape that I needed for a project. I took it out," he said, mimicking taking out a big roll of tape. "Took off a piece, and taped his mouth shut." I looked at him, surprised. "Didn't you get in trouble?" I asked. He shook his head, chuckling faintly. "Not at all. Everyone was thanking me," he said. I looked at Aaron and found he was chuckling softly at the memory, too.

"Where's Severin?" I asked, finding him nowhere around here. "Behind you," Severin said, cupping his warm hands around my eyes. "Nice to see you," I said, grabbing his arm and pulling him down next to me. For a fleeting moment, I saw something on Steve's face. It looked like disappointment, or something close to that. But it went away as soon as it came as he opened the pizza box. Something in me tugged painfully, and for a few frightening moments, I thought my wings wanted to burst free again. Then I realized that I felt something, too. Guilt, I think. *Well, I can't think about it now* I said as a triangular slice of droopy pizza was handed to me.

*　　*　　*

49

Later that night, Steve and Aaron brought us some water for the night. "There's no running water in the house, and you guys look pretty dirty," Aaron said casually, a bucket of water on the floor next to him. Steve looked at him sharply and shook his head. "I mean dirty in the not sexy way," Aaron said immediately, covering up his mistake. I have found Steve to be looking at me a lot lately. I tried to ignore it, but found that impossible, since I would occasionally look at him, too.

"Well, I guess I'll see you tomorrow," Steve said, mostly looking at me. "Maybe we'll get you guys some new clothes tomorrow. It must've been a while since you had any real clothes." He turned to leave, then looked at us both. "You guys will have to tell me how you managed to survive out there. It must be pretty cold out there. Not to mention the lack of food," he said, then left out of the door behind Aaron without a goodbye.

Severin looked at me. "Which room do you want?" he asked. "It doesn't matter," I said, walking over to the water bucket. I splashed some water on my face and scrubbed roughly with a rag. I looked at the once white cloth and saw how filthy it was.

"You should wash up," I said, handing him a white rag. His face was a little dirty, with mud streaks across his cheeks and dirt in patches and clumps along his face. He took the rag and dipped it in the water. I watched as he cleaned his face with rough strokes that left a red mark on his skin.

I shook my head. "Here, let me get that for you," I said, taking the rag from his face before he could inflict any more damage. "You are too rough with your face," I said and gently began to stroke his face with the rag. It took a while, but the dirt and mud eventually came off. Severin looked into my eyes and grabbed my hand on his face.

"You know," he said, "You are kind of amazing." "What do you mean?" I asked him, beginning to feel small and weak under his gaze. He leaned closer, and I shrunk back. "You always seem to know when danger is near, and you know how to survive. I've only been alive for three days, but you already treat me like family. Maybe even more," he said, his thumb stroking my left cheek. "Thank you for that," he whispered. I stood speechless as he leaned down and kissed me softly on my lips. I kissed him back just as soft. He began to deepen the kiss, his hand moving from my cheek to the back of my head. Emotion swirled through me as I dropped the rag and moved my hands to the back of his head. I grabbed his hair and pulled him closer to me. His hands moved from my head to my waist and touched the bare skin where my shirt had ridden up. Heat shot up from his hand and raced along my spine. I gasped against his lips. It felt wonderful, this tingling heat.

All of a sudden, Steve entered my mind. I don't know why, but it was enough make me realize what was going on with Severin and where this could lead to. "Severin, stop," I said, pulling away. He stopped kissing me, but his nose was still touching mine. "I'm sorry," he said, his eyes like pools of blue silver. "Did I hurt you?" "No," I answered, "I just don't think this is the time or place." He just looked at me. "Am I moving too fast?" he asked, his voice almost a whisper. "Maybe," I answered honestly. "Like you said, you are only three days old, versus me, with five weeks."

He pulled his face away but kept his hands on my back. "Did I move too fast when we kissed earlier?" "Probably," I said shrugging out of his embrace. "I don't want to talk about it right now. Let's get to bed," I said, turning to the closest room available.

"Goodnight, Violet," he said softly from behind me. "Goodnight, Severin," I responded. I closed the door from behind me and looked at my new room. It had one of the best things I had ever seen. A real bed.

Back at the lab, I slept on the wooden floor of my crate. Last night, I had slept in a hole made of dirt. Tonight, for the first time, I was going to sleep on a real bed. Excitement rippled through me as I jumped on the bed. I rolled onto my stomach and took off my shirt to stretch my wings. The bones in them cracked with relief as they massaged themselves. I allowed them some space to move as I lay on my back underneath the covers. The bed was a bit squeaky, but extremely comfortable. I laid my head on the pillow and fell into a deep sleep in no time.

*   *   *

"Hey, can I come in?" Severin asked softly, scaring the living daylights out of me. It had to be midnight, but there was a heavy rain and thunder shaking the old house. Lightening flashed startling white light through the windows, illuminating the entire room.

"Sure," I said, opening the covers to him and hoping he would ignore the fact that I was half-naked. He slithered inside just as another bolt of lightening and thunder struck, shaking the entire house. Severin curled up next to me, and with a sudden realization I found he was shaking.

"Severin, are you scared of storms?" I asked. "I don't know," he said, his arms around my back and his head buried inside my chest. He was shaking so hard that I began to shake. I hugged him and pulled him close. He was only three days old, and was still beginning to discover the world, so that pretty much gave him every right to want to be with me at night. *He is so much like a small child* I thought to myself as he tugged me closer when thunder struck again.

"It's okay, Severin," I said. "I'll protect you from the scary monsters of the storm." "Ha ha," he said sarcastically against my chest. His warm body covered mine in a perfect fit. Suddenly, I thought of something. "Severin," I asked softly. "Do you think we may have met each other before we turned into mutants?" "I don't know," he said thoughtfully. "But I will admit that you looked familiar to me when I first saw you. I thought it was just what the workers did to me, but it went deeper than that," he said. I thought about what he said. He sure did bring strange emotions in me, like I should remember something that was no longer there.

"Well, let's get to sleep," I said. "Okay," Severin said. After about an hour of him jumping every time thunder erupted, he finally fell asleep. I stayed awake a little longer, thinking. I knew he wanted us to be more than just friends, but he was more of a little brother to me than anything, no matter how great of a kisser he was. I thought of Steve, and how he would look at me every now and then, especially when Severin sat next to me. He seemed so disappointed, like he wished he was sitting next to me instead of Severin. I sighed and, leaning into Severin's warmth, fell into a light sleep with only the pounding rain and booming thunder sounding throughout the night.

Chapter Eight

I awoke the next morning with the sound of Severin's breathing in my ear. Sometime during the night, I had shifted with my back towards him. His arms were still around me, and he was pressed gently against my back. A quick look out the window revealed a bright sunshine, showing no proof of the raging storm that had taken place last night. Birds called to each other outside, creating a peaceful mood throughout the house.

I carefully disengaged Severin's arms from around my waist, trying not to wake him. I got off of the bed, put my shirt on, and looked at him. He was sleeping like a dead man, as if all of the exercise of walking and basketball had drained all of his energy yesterday. I bent down and stroked his hair; I just couldn't help it. He was just so much like a child, a mere infant, in this new life. A surge of affectionate warmth rolled through me as I pulled away from him and, trying not to make the floors creak too much, went out the open door.

The living room was lighted by the sunlight coming out through the stained glass windows near the entrance door and windows throughout the house. I looked out of the backyard window.

The grass on the outside was wet and mushy, and mud covered the bottom of the fence surrounding the backyard. There was a single giant oak tree covering most of the house with a little swing beneath it. An abandoned basketball sat near the tree trunk, dirty and worn, and in desperate need of an air pump.

I tore myself away from the window and settled next to the water bucket. I took a long, thirsty drink and sat down. I heard the sounds of Severin waking up in the bedroom, and in no time, he was sitting right besides me.

"Good morning," I said to him. "Morning," he said, his voice raspy from sleep. His hair was bedraggled, and his eyes were still soft from sleep. "Drink some water," I said. "Your voice is cracking." He obliged happily.

There was a knock at the door. "It's me," Steve's voice called. He opened the unlocked door and entered the living room, carrying a duffle bag.

"I thought you had school," I said to him as he took a seat on the lumpy couch besides me.

"I ditched," he said, rolling his eyes, acting like it was the most obvious thing in the world. "Okay," I said. "And where is your partner in crime?" He smiled. "I thought you guys could take a break from him," he said. "But enough about Aaron. You guys could really use some new clothes," he said, unzipping the duffle bag and pulling out two sets of clothes. "I think mine might be too big for Severin, but it should do," he said, tossing Severin his new clothes. "And as for you," he said, turning to me. "I just stole some of my mom's. I think they'll fit perfectly." He tossed me the clothes.

"Thanks," I said, offering him a smile. He beamed at my acceptance. "I'll go change," I said, getting up. Once inside my room, I took a look at my clothes. The shirt was black with a white lotus flower on the front, and the jeans looked old and ragged. But Steve was right—they fit me perfectly. I walked out and showed off my new outfit. "You were right, Steve," I said, "There're just my size." "Good, I thought they would," Steve said. "Come sit with me," he said, patting the spot next to him. Severin was nowhere to be found, so I assumed that he was getting dressed. The couch sank under my weight as I sat down and forced me to lean into Steve.

"Sorry," I said, fighting the blush creeping up my cheeks. "Not a problem," he said, and before I could move away, he put his arm around me. I froze in place as my eyes grew wide, his warmth seeping into my shoulders. I must've made a strange face, because Steve laughed and removed his arm. "Am I making you uncomfortable?" he asked, my body still pressed against his. My shoulders cried out to be touched by his skin again, but I knew that I shouldn't desire his touch.

"No," I said, and tried to get away from his body. Just then, Severin entered the room. "Whoa, am I interrupting something?" he asked, looking us both up and down. "No," I said, getting up from the couch. Severin looked undeniably handsome in those dark blue jeans and plain black shirt. It really complemented his eyes.

"Are we ready to go?" I asked Steve, walking over to Severin and allowing him the pleasure of putting his arm around me. "Not yet," he answered. "It's too early. People are going to wonder why we aren't in school. We'll have to wait until after lunch. That way, it'll seem like we were home schooled." I had no idea what he was talking about, so I just nodded. Steve brightened. "Hey, Severin, you want to play football? I can teach you if you like," he said, pulling out an oddly shaped brown ball from his bag.

"I don't know," Severin said, though he looked at the ball with greedy desire. "Is it like basketball?" "No, but it's just as fun," Steve said.

I looked at Severin. "Go play. I'll watch," I said. Severin removed his arm from around me and practically ran to the backyard door to follow Steve. "Boys," I muttered under my breath. "Oh, Violet," Steve said, poking his head out the door. "I brought a portable DVD player with some movies. You can watch those if you like." "Thanks," I said as he walked out of the door.

I had no clue what a DVD was, so I went into my room and sat down on the bed. It was still surprisingly warm from this morning. I took off my shirt and looked at my dark green scales. They shined like polished glass and made small rainbows when it caught the light. They may have looked cold, but they were warm and felt like snake skin when I touched them. My wings stretched out until the bones cracked, giving me a pleasurable feeling in my back. I sighed with relief and lay on my back. A sharp pain in my right ankle made me sit up quickly. I looked under my sock and found that I had forgotten to remove my knife. I took it out and examined the blade. One side of it was warm from my skin and had a small red line of dried blood trailing along its edge. I touched the rust-colored blood, wondering how it got there.

A shattering of glass interrupted my thoughts. "Steve? Severin?" I called out. "Is everything okay?" No answer. Then Severin cried, "Violet! Help!" My heart bumping against my chest, I willed my wings to retract and yanked on my shirt as I ran out into the backyard and crashed into something really big and ugly.

It had to be at least thirty feet tall. It had slimy green skin and arms with something like branches sticking out at unattractive angles. Three eyes, one on its nose, stared at me with hungry intensity. But worst of all was the putrid smell leaking out of its open pores in both a gas and a liquid.

"Severin?" I asked as the creepy monster advanced slowly on me. "Where is Steve?" "He fainted," he said, his voice a frightened whisper.

"Hello, *mutant*," the monster said, it's voice a feminine sneer. Build was freaky, but her vibes weren't very scary. As a matter of fact, her vibes seemed frightened instead of frightening. Strange, but that didn't stop it—her—from swinging her arm at me, her three sharp, yellow, foot-long claws extended to full length. I jumped back just as her claws whistled in the empty air that used to be me.

"Severin!" I yelled. "Grab Steve and run away as fast as you can. I'll catch up," I said as the monster took another swing at me. I jumped back just as Severin lunged onto the monster's back.

"Severin! Run away!" I screamed when the monster started to thrash around. She bucked like a horse, and Severin flew off of her back and landed facedown on the wet grass with a hard *thump*.

"I'm not leaving you!" Severin said when the monster turned to him. "Fools!" the monster sneered. "I am here to take you back to the lab you so luckily escaped from. I am stronger than the two of you combined. You can't defeat me!" Was it just me, or did she sound unsure? She let loose a raspy laugh and swung her claws at Severin. "Severin, look out!" I cried.

He had surprisingly quick reflexes for someone so young. He gracefully jumped out of the way as I released my claws and ran towards the smelly beast. Instead of trying to get on her back, I targeted her feet. I sliced open the tendons on the back of her feet, the unusual, foul smelling yellow dust clouding the area around them. She howled with pain as she collapsed on the ground besides me. "I'll kill you!" she screeched as she unsuccessfully tried to get up.

Not one to waste time, I climbed onto her big slimy stomach—though I may have slipped a few times—and bore my claws to her throat. "Get off of me," she said, and tried to hit me with her ugly claws. Luckily for me, Severin had wasted no time at all and held her hands together above her head.

She immediately saw that she was outnumbered and forced herself to relax against my claws as they dug into her throat.

"Why are you here?" I asked her, hardening my voice and not releasing my claws. "I am here to bring you back to the lab," she said resentfully. Her awful smell was clogging up my nose, and I had a horrible urge to gag. I resisted the possibility and asked the next question.

"Are you from the lab around here?" "Yes," she said, and I noticed a slight tremor in her voice. "I used to be normal. But they experimented on me and now look at me. I'm hideous!" she wailed. A small shiver ran up my spine and my blood started to slow. "What did they do to you?" I asked, my voice beginning to shake, pity for this ugly creature starting to bubble in my chest.

"They stole me from the streets. They hurt me, put things into me. I was only seven, and they took me away!" she said, her face contorting as sobs racked her entire body. "They sent me after you to bring you back there. They wanted to do bad things to you, just like they did to me. I don't want to hurt you. Don't make me go back there!" she cried, nearly throwing me off of her stomach. Then, with a sudden jolt, the monster began to shrink. "Violet, what's going on?" Severin asked as the monster began to shift and form into a different shape. She shrank until my own body covered hers completely. I rolled off of her and took a good, long look at her. Her slimy green skin melted away to reveal soft human skin. Silky blonde hair sprouted from her head and her eyes changed from a harsh, ugly brown to a gentle green.

"Whoa!" Severin said as her arms changed color from green to pale white and slipped through his hands. The girl looked seemingly normal, except for the bloody tendons in her feet that now seemed to be healing themselves.

"See what I mean?" she said. I stared at her, opened mouthed. "How did you do that? What are you?" I asked her, forcing my claws back into my fingers and pulling her up besides me. She looked young, even younger than me. She shook her head. "Now isn't the place to talk about it," she said. "We need to get out of here. They can still track me down when I'm outside." I looked to the house. "Go inside the house. I'll catch up," I told her. She looked at me gratefully and entered the house.

"Violet," Severin said. "What did you just do?" "I have no clue," I said. I met his blue gaze. "Where's Steve?" "Right here," he said, pointing downward. I flinched when I saw him. He had a large bump on his head and was lying sideways on the grass.

"That looks like it would hurt," I said as I bent down and examined the bump on Steve's head. It was a shiny pink, and a small cut marred his left cheek, but other than that, he was fine. "Get inside, Severin," I said as he turned and left.

I trusted that the girl in the house wasn't going to hurt him; her vibes were too gentle. Besides, with her lanky build, even Severin could take her easily if she decided to attack.

And, okay, maybe her innocence made me want to give her a second chance. It just seemed like the right thing to do at the moment. She could be useful if another mutant tried to capture us.

I gently put my arm under Steve's legs and neck and, very carefully, picked him up. He was surprisingly light for his size, so I had no trouble carrying him to the house. His skin was warm against mine, and hot tingles crept along my arms where his skin touched me. He looked peaceful in sleep, and I resisted the strong urge to touch his face. I forced myself to look away as I carried him over the threshold. Once inside, I shooed Severin from the couch and placed him there. The girl was sitting on the hard floor next to Severin.

I looked at Steve one last time and turned to her. "Okay, first is first, what is your name?" I said, my eyes prodding hers. "Number thirty-two," she said, looking down at her hands, looking miserable. I cocked my head, confused. "What do you mean 'number thirty-two'?" I asked her. "The people at the lab didn't bother giving us real names, and since I'm subject number thirty-two, that's what they called me," she said, though she seemed just as confused as me. "Don't you have a number?" she asked.

"No," I said. "Aaron, well, the workers, gave us human names. Mine is Violet, and his is Severin," I said, pointing to him. "What about him?" she asked, pointing to Steve. "He's not a mutant," I said. "His name is Steve, and he's a normal human." She looked stunned. "But he saw me," she said. "I let him see me in mutant form. What will he think when he wakes up?"

I thought for a moment. "I don't know," I said, the realization crashing into me. What *will* he think? He would surely want an explanation when he wakes up. What will I tell him? I tried not to think about it as I continued my interrogation.

"Are there more of you?" I asked, walking over to Severin and sitting down next to him. "Yes," she said. "But I am the youngest in both physical and mutant life. I was seven when they took me off the streets, and I am currently one year old in mutant life. But what species are you?" she asked. "I have no clue. We're too new, I guess," I said.

"What can we call you?" Severin interrupted. He looked down. "Well, I sure don't want to call you thirty-two. How about a real name?" he said.

Just then, Steve groaned from the couch. Severin looked at me, his eyes wide and alarmed. Panicking, I shot up from the floor and knelt next to Steve. He groaned again and slowly opened his eyes.

"Where am I?" he asked painfully, looking around him. Before I could respond, he jumped up into a sitting position and looked at Severin. "What was that?" he asked Severin, his voice raising a few octaves. "There was this really ugly thing-," "Okay," I interrupted. "That, um, football hit your head pretty hard. You were probably seeing things," I told him, the lie slipping surprisingly easily from my lips. He just stared at me. "But I didn't get hit. It appeared out of *nowhere!*" he said, and tried to get up. I pushed him back down gently until his head hit the pillows.

"Don't tell me you didn't see it," he told Severin. Then he looked at me. "What's going on here?" I didn't want to tell him the truth; it would be too great for him to understand. All I could do was hope that he would believe me when I told him it was all in his head.

"No, I saw the ball hit your head. You just hallucinated," I told him. Severin agreed. Steve hesitated for a moment.

"Okay . . ." he said, but he looked as if he didn't believe us. He suddenly looked over my shoulder.

"Who is that?" he asked me, pointing his finger to a small foot poking out from behind the chair. "That's . . . Candy," I told him, saying the first name that came to mind. "She was with us yesterday. Don't you remember her?" I said quickly, trying to make my voice convincing. Candy cautiously came out from behind the chair and stood next to me. "Don't you remember me?" she asked in her soft voice.

"No," he said, as though trying not to hurt her feelings. "All I remember is Violet and Severin. Sorry though," he said, staring at her face as though trying to remember her. "Man, I must've hit my head really hard," he said, and attempted to sit up again, only to have me push him down.

"You need to rest," I said, trying to make him believe my lie. "You have a really bad bump on your head. I'll clean you up." Severin and Candy left the room while I tended to Steve. I used one of our old rags and pressed it gently to his wound.

The scratch wasn't much more than a minor flesh wound, and the swelling in his bump was going down, so I took that as a good sign. "See, it's not so bad," I told him. He grabbed my hand, sending the usual hot tingles up my arm.

"Tell me the truth," he said. "Was there really a monster out there?" I sighed, knowing he won't buy my story. "No, there wasn't," I said, pulling my hand from his grasp and trying to sound convincing. He wasn't about to let me go that easily. As I turned to get a cleaner rag, he grabbed my other hand and pulled me next to him on the couch.

"Steve," I said as he wrapped his arms around me and pulled me against his chest. "I don't believe you," he said. "I really don't remember Candy, and I know I didn't get hit with a football. Tell me what's going on," he said, his lips close to my ear. I was so hot I was almost panting. The tingle was everywhere. My head was almost buried into his neck, his smell surrounding me. Soap, I thought. He smelled like soap. And cloud, if there was even a scent for it.

His lips grazed from my ear to my cheek. "Tell me," he whispered, his lips now almost at my own lips. I gasped as the hot tingles turned to a raging fire in my veins and on my skin. I wanted him to kiss me. Right now. "No, Steve," I said, and pulled away from him. I quickly got off the couch and practically ran to my room, slamming the door behind me.

This wasn't right. I kissed Severin twice. We were meant to be together, right? I touched my cheek where Steve had rested his lips. I could still feel them there, waiting for me to make the next move. *But he doesn't even like me* I thought. He was just trying to get seduce information out of me. I sat down on my bed, trying to control my breathing.

"Hey, can I come in?" Candy asked through my door. "Sure," I said as the door opened and she walked in. "Close the door behind you," I instructed. "Okay," she said, closing the door and sitting next to me on the bed.

"Where's Severin?" I asked. "In his room," she said. She looked at me with sad eyes. "He saw you with Steve and got jealous, so he won't come out of his room." "Oh, great," I said, plopping down against the bed and closing my eyes. The last thing I needed was a jealous, four day old boy breathing down my back.

"Thanks for the cover-up back there," she said. "Candy. That's a pretty name." "I just said the first thing that came to mind," I said, blushing. "There's no need to thank me." We were quiet for a while.

"They can find me if I'm outside," she said suddenly, breaking the silence. "What do you mean?" I asked her, getting into a sitting position. She looked guilty, almost remorseful. "They put some kind of scanner inside me to tell where I am. The only good thing about it is that it doesn't work when I have a roof over my head," she said in one breath. I just looked at her.

"I tried to tell you earlier," she said defensively, seeing my stunned look. "But if that's true . . . ," I began.

"Then if I step out of this house, they'll know exactly where I am," she finished for me. I leaned back onto the pillows, shocked. If she walked outside, the people would find not only her, but us as well. There was always the possibility of leaving Candy here while Severin and I made a run for it, but I wasn't about to let this young girl get captured again. I trusted her, for some strange reason, and felt strangely protective of her.

"Where is the scanner?" I asked. "Right here," she said, pulling up her pink shirt and turning around. I gasped at the gruesome sight. There, attached to her spine with the skin of her back growing around it, was a small black ball with an occasional red light flashing out every three seconds. Blood and puss oozed out continuously around the edges, and it looked as if it could easily get infected.

The worst part? The wound looked fresh.

"That . . . looks like it hurts," I said, barely managing the words. Rage built inside me. If this is what the humans at the lab did to this poor little girl, then what were they going to do to me and Severin?

"It throbs from time to time," she said. "I can't see it, though, so I guess by your voice that it must look worse than it feels." "No kidding," I said, touching the ball and feeling the need to gag. "I don't know if you can help me, but if you can, please do so," she said sheepishly.

"There is," I said. "Really?" she asked, turning to face me, her expression hopeful. "You can set me free?" "Yes," I said. "But it will hurt like hell."

"I don't care," she said, yanking her shirt off. "Do it." I flinched at what she wanted me to do. "Uh, can you get Severin here first," I asked unconvincingly. "I'll need his help." Actually, I just needed some company. "Sure, sure," she said, running out of the room with her shirt still off. The door was wide open, and I saw Steve on the couch, asleep, in the exact same position as I had left him. I quickly looked away, blushing. I didn't know he was shirtless.

Two seconds later, Candy and Severin entered the room. Severin didn't look too happy, and seemed to be avoiding eye contact with me. Sigh. I guess I wouldn't blame him, after what he saw.

"Severin?" I asked. "What?" he asked, making me wince at the hint of harshness in his voice. "Can you go and get the bucket and the rest of the clean rags?" I asked, deciding to ignore his tone. "Sure," he said, and walked out of the room.

"He doesn't know what is going to happen, does he?" I asked Candy. "Nope," she said, a little too excited for the extreme pain about to come upon her. "Okay, so I'm going to need you to lie on the bed on your stomach," I told her. She obliged happily. Just then, Severin came into the room. "Here," he said, still not looking at me, though, thankfully, the harsh tone was gone.

"Now, Severin," I said. "Close your eyes." He looked at me curiously, but did as he asked. I turned to Candy. "Bite that pillow," I said. "Okay," she said, swiftly placing the pillow in her mouth. "Okay," I breathed as I unsheathed my claws and fought back a wave of nausea. *Be brave* I told myself as I began to pick the ball out of her back.

* * *

Candy acted surprisingly well as my claws dug into her spine. Sure, there was a lot of blood, but the rags took good care of that; plus, her skin started to heal immediately. She would whimper in pain every now and then, but the ball came out easily. Sometime during the homemade surgery, Severin had sat next to me on the bed and watched me work my gory magic.

"Is it out?" Candy asked when I finished. "Yes," I told her. She beamed and hugged me before flinching at the pain from the hole in her back. "You better lie down," I told her, showing her the round hunk of metal that had tracked her every move. "That's okay," she said. "I have unbelievable healing abilities. My immune system is so strong, I can't even get sick," she said, putting on her shirt.

Severin helped me pick up the bloody rags and stashed them under the bed, hoping Steve and Aaron wouldn't notice three rags were missing. "Well, I would feel better if you would lie down," I said. "Fine," she said, and snuggled under the covers. She was asleep within seconds.

"That was fast," Severin whispered to me. "Talk about," I muttered back, and started to make my way to the living room.

"Wait," Severin said, grabbing my arm. "What's going on with you and Steve?" I thought for a moment, thinking of a way to explain. "If you want to be with him, then that's okay," he said, releasing my arm. "It's okay with me."

"No, Severin," I said, walking up close to him. "He didn't believe my story. He was just trying to seduce me so I would tell him the truth," I said. He looked unconvinced. "Will this prove it?" I asked, and pressed my lips to his. He didn't respond at first, but then started to kiss me back, softly at first, then with much more passion. His hands roamed along my waist, then closed around my back. He groaned, pulling me closer. And just like that, my small, friendly kiss turned into something a lot more passionate.

"Severin, wait," I gasped. "Hm?" he asked, sensually moving his lips to my cheek and nibbling on the bottom of my jaw. "We have an audience," I said, forcing myself away from his body and gesturing towards the bed where Candy lay asleep. "Right," he said, his voice husky and low. "Sorry."

"Hey, I started it this time," I said to his benefit. He chuckled. "Yeah, please do that more often," he said, pulling me close to him again. He kissed me once more on my lips and left the room.

"Where is all that smacking noise coming from?" Candy asked groggily from the bed. I froze. "Uh, nowhere," I told her. "It's all in your head."

"Right," she said sarcastically as she went back to sleep.

Chapter Nine

"What are we going to tell Steve?" I asked Severin as he gathered up his old clothes and placed them in a plastic bag he found under the bed. "We'll just tell him that we need to get going. It's not like he was expecting us to stay for more than a day," he said.

Severin wanted us to leave this place. Just him, me, and Candy. What can I say; he seemed to be warming up to the kid. But I really didn't want to leave this place; I liked it here. "But why do we have to leave so soon?" I asked him as he stood up to face me. "Well, maybe because the guys at the lab probably know where we are. They'll begin to suspect something if Candy doesn't show up soon, so we need to leave before they can get any idea where we are," he said, looking down at me.

I sighed. "But we still need to find a place for us to stay, unless you want to sleep under an oversized trash can again," I said in his face. It was his turn to sigh. "We will just make do with what we've got." I stared at him. "But what about Candy? She's just a child! You don't expect her to just willingly go wherever we want her to, especially if we can't take care of her" I shot.

"I think you've forgot that she grew up in a lab, same as you. I think she'll be willing to go anywhere we want in the name of freedom," he said, and turned away from me. "Get your things. We're leaving in a few minutes."

Rage boiled inside of me as I left the room, sputtering profanities that Aaron taught me in the lab when he got frustrated at me. I looked at Steve as I entered the living room. He stirred and yawned.

"Violet?" he asked when he opened his eyes. "Why are you leaving so early?" he asked me curiously. I froze, shell shocked. "How did you know?" I asked him. He smiled. "You and Severin weren't being too quiet in there." Then he turned serious. "Why are you leaving?"

I looked down and bit my lip. "Severin wants to go. He thinks someone from back home might know where we are. He doesn't want to risk getting caught," I admitted guiltily. Steve was silent for a moment.

"Do you want to leave?" he asked me silently. "No," I responded. "But Severin's right; we don't want to be found. We're leaving in a few minutes," I said, and turned and left Steve there. I gathered up my clothes and woke Candy up.

"So soon?" she asked after I told her the news. "Yes. Severin's ready." "Okay," she said, and got up from the bed. "You know," she said as she neared the door, "He doesn't want to leave just because of that. He also wants to keep you away from Steve." Then she left to meet Severin.

I just stood there, stunned. Why would Severin want to do that? I kissed him myself, didn't I? Didn't that kiss prove that I wasn't going behind his back? A sudden knock at the door interrupted my thoughts.

"Hey," Steve said as he entered the room. "Hey," I said, walking up to him. I could tell he was upset, but he masked his feelings well. "I came to tell you guys that it would be best if you leave in about two hours. It would just seem strange if people saw you guys walking around during school hours," he said. "Thanks for the tip," I said. "I'll tell Severin that." I began to walk out of the room when Steve grabbed my arm. "I know this isn't the right time, but after all of that time walking around, all the way from Canada, why are you so ready to get back on the road again when you finally have a roof over your heads? It's not like you've had any place to stay for quite some time."

"Well," I started, but Steve kept talking. "And what about Candy? She's still too young to be running from the law or whatever you three are involved in," he said. I said nothing for a minute, trying to figure out what to say. Then, "You really think we are running from the law?"

Steve blushed and looked down. "Well, I don't know why you three don't want to be found. I mean, besides the fact that you and Severin are supposed to do something you don't want to do, but still, what does Candy have to do with all of this?" he kept babbling on.

I hung my head. "You won't let me go unless I tell you everything, won't you?" I asked him. "Yep," he said, sitting on the bed and patting the spot next to him. I sat down beside him. "Okay, here's the truth," I said softly. "Candy is my sister. My parents wanted Severin and me to, uh, rob a bank, and they wanted Candy to watch us do it." I said. He just stared at me.

"They wanted you to rob a bank?" he asked incredulously, as if he didn't believe me. "It's true," I said, trying anything to make him believe me. "Right," he said, and got off the bed. He turned toward the door. "I can tell when you're lying. When you are ready to tell me the truth, well, you know where to find me." Then he left without another word.

*　　*　　*

Two hours later, Severin, Candy, and I were all packed up and ready to hit the road once more.

"Thanks for letting us borrow the house," Severin told Steve as we left the neighborhood and entered the city beyond. "No problem," Steve said, slapping him on the back.

"Promise me you guys will visit again. Next time, Aaron and I can teach you how to wrestle." Severin and Steve kept talking while Candy and I explored our surroundings.

The city was boisterous, full of loud energy. Humans were everywhere, in cars, on the sidewalk, in the buildings, even sharing the road with the cars.

"This place is huge!" Candy exclaimed, tugging on my hand and pointing at one of the parked cars. "What is that?" "A car," I said, fighting the urge to laugh. She has been acting just like a kid in a toy shop ever since we arrived in the city, pointing out things and asking me to name them. It was kind of sad, actually, to find that I had learned more than her in five weeks while she was alive for an entire year and learned nothing of the outside world.

"Hey, Violet," Steve said, jarring me from my thoughts. "Yes?" "Thanks." I looked at him, confused. "Why are you thanking me?" "I don't know. You just seem to make my day when I see you. I know I'm going to miss you," he said, then looked down.

"Thanks for saying that," I told him. He smiled and offered his hand. I shook it, the hot tingles racing up my arm the moment I touched him. But this time, he didn't let go immediately. "Okay you two. Let's go," Candy said, grabbing my free hand and Severin. "Bye, Steve," I said as I was pulled along by Candy and Severin.

"Goodbye, Violet," he murmured, and waved at us. Severin grabbed my other hand and pulled me along with Candy.

"Alright, so where are we going?" Candy asked a few blocks later. "I don't know," Severin said. "Violet's driving." "Hey, who said anything about me driving?" I asked. "I thought we were just running from the lab." "Uh, we better get going, if that's the case," Candy said, pointing at a television shop. Some of the TVs were broadcasting the news in the window. "Oh my God," I said when I saw my own face on the television.

"As we all know, there was a robbery at the Western lab in Canada that had taken place a few days ago," someone said in the background. "Police had finally discovered the thieves right here in Wisconsin. There has obviously been a secret lab in the woods where they worked on experiments involving missing children, all of which were found dead on the scene. However, when the FBI arrested the people involved with the crime, they found that the two teens from Canada escaped, along with one of the children from the lab missing. Security camera footage shows the two of them flying over the fence."

All three of us gasped when the television rolled the tape of the both me and Severin flying over the fence. We were in black and white, and the camera quality wasn't good, but you could still see the scales on our bodies, and our claws were out. But the scariest thing of all was our wings.

They stretched out like bat wings and soared through the air, almost dragon like against the gray sky.

"Recently found documents in the Western lab reveal the two teens' names and age. The girl's name is Violet, and she is currently thirty nine days old, and the boy's name is Severin, and he was only alive for four days. They were under the care of Aaron Richard, who had somehow survived the attack, but at the price of life—threatening injuries to his body. The doctors don't think he will survive with his fatal wounds. Although he is undergoing several medications to keep him alive, he was able to reveal what classification the mutants are."

Then they showed a picture of Aaron lying in a hospital bed. I wanted to hurl when I saw him. He looked horrible with those white casts clinging to his arms and legs. A bloodstained bandage was tied around his head, and his left eye was swollen and black. He had multiple bruises along his face, and his lips were chapped.

"They are a part of an ancient race called the Dragon Kin," Aaron said, his voice dry and raspy. "We didn't experiment on them. They were born this way. The only thing we did to them was introduce their bodies to their ancestors' blood. It was said to awaken the Dragon Kin. There is a prophecy that speaks of a time that when the end of the world arrives, the Dragon Kin would save the humans from the apocalypse. The reason they hadn't seemed to exist over the past couple of years was because of the Dragon Kin Hunters. Ever since they came to earth, they began to slay the Dragon Kin. From then on, the numbers of Dragon Kin decreased rapidly." He paused.

"By the second century, all of the Dragon Kin were thought to be extinct. But they were not. You see, my father and mother are Dragon Kin, which left me to be one as well. The Dragon Kin had learned how to shift into human form, and were able to live in the human world. They can only breed with their own kind, which would mean that Severin and Violet are pureblood Dragon Kin. Violet's and Severin's parents both died when they were little, and Violet was put into foster care at the age of three, all thanks to a secret society that still kills the Dragon Kin. Severin was still being studied, so we don't know much about his heritage. However, I do know that, since my own parents died a few years back, that there are currently three male Dragon Kin and one female in the entire world. I know for a fact that Violet is the last remaining female, and that Severin and I are two of the last male Dragon Kin.

"According to my research, the last male should be somewhere in the United States. The Dragon Kin aren't dangerous, but I know that Violet could put up a good fight," he said, and chuckled brokenly. I just wanted to faint.

"The reason the other lab wanted them was because they thought they could make them purely human. But that's impossible," he said, and the screen went back to the people talking. "If you see these two teens, contact the authorities immediately, and do not approach them directly," one woman said, and the screen showed a full head picture of us in color.

Severin looked at me, his mouth hanging open. "The Dragon Kin? What is that supposed to be?" he whispered. I shook my head, feeling the need to throw up.

Aaron was alive! I couldn't believe it. But what did he mean we were the "Dragon Kin"? I remember that Aaron told me stories about them when I was three days old, but I thought they were just a myth. He told me about "responsibilities" that I must endure, but he never told me that saving the world was one of them!

"Uh, guys," Candy prodded suddenly. "We had better get going. There are people staring at us." Severin and I turned around and saw three people looking at us curiously. Then they gasped when they saw our faces.

"It's them!" one woman said, pulling out her cell phone. "No, don't call the police," I said desperately. I really didn't want to get caught, especially when they saw Candy. I wasn't too sure what they were going to do to her. And I wasn't about to find out.

"Run!" I yelled, and started burning the pavement with my shoes. Severin and Candy weren't too far behind me. We ran a few blocks and hid next to a building to catch our breaths. "What are we going to do?" Severin asked between pants. "Get out of here, obviously," I said. "We need to get out of the city," Candy pointed out. "I know. Where is the exit over here?" Severin said, looking around us. Humans were everywhere, so I was surprised that none of them paid any attention to us. Then again, it was a little early for them to know who we were.

"Excuse me," someone said behind me, pushing me aside and walking up to a telephone pole. The man had a stack of papers and tape in his hand. I watched as he took one of the papers and taped it to the pole. He hurried away and seemed to find another pole two blocks over. "What is that?" Severin asked, walking up to the poster.

"Uh, Violet," Severin suddenly said. "We really need to get out of here. They have wanted posters of us." "What?" I quickly made my way to Severin. "Oh, great," I said, disgusted. There, on that poster, was a drawing of me and Severin, our horns visible through our hair and our scales showing a little too far up on our necks. Our eyes were slits, and our expressions malevolent.

"Do I really look like that?" I asked Severin, touching my cheeks. "Not really," he said, though he kept looking between me and my picture.

"Now isn't the time, guys," Candy said, remorse creeping into her voice. "We're about to have company." I heard gasps and yelps from behind me, and I turned around to see a group of people standing there, looking at me and Severin.

"Oh my god, it's them!" One said. Several of them took out their cell phones and started dialing. The rest of them scattered like frightened deer. I began to panic. "Run," I said to Severin, and took his hand. I grabbed Candy's arm as I passed by her and took off running as fast as my exhausted legs would carry me.

"Damn, how big is this place?" I gasped as we fell against a tree in a nearby park. The bark was a little frosted, and it seemed to be about ten degrees cooler under its shade. The cold air stung my throat and I could see my breath in small puffs of white smoke. "If we keep going in one direction, we should be able to reach the end of the city," Candy said, her voice almost a whisper from exhaustion. "Well, lets rest for a little bit," Severin said, putting his arms around both me and Candy's shoulders. They were cold at first, but their warmth seeped in slowly, and I leaned into him, as did Candy. "We are going to need some warmer clothing, and soon," Candy said after a while. "Yeah," Severin agreed. "I don't know how we will survive the night."

Just then, we heard police sirens outside of the park, driving recklessly towards the place where the group of people saw us. "Well, at least the police didn't see us," Candy said, her head resting against Severin's shoulder. I sighed and did the same thing. A dark, unsettling feeling began in the pit of my stomach. A lighted sign on a store caught my eye on my right.

"Donate your old worn clothes for charity!" Someone next to the store said. On his left was a big pile of old coats and jackets, along with some long sleeved shirts and sweatpants. Shoes and fluffy socks dominated the ground beneath the wheelbarrow of clothes.

"Guys, I have an idea," I said, my mood beginning to brighten in this cold, heartless city.

Chapter Ten

"That was easy," Candy said as we made our way out of the park with our new used socks, jackets, and sweatpants. While the man working the booth wasn't looking, all three of us ran and took what seemed would fit us. Severin now carried a blue jacket almost the exact color of his scales, along with black sweatpants and dark green socks. Candy was lucky enough to snatch a light pink jacket with cute swirling designs, along with light purplish-pink sweatpants and azure colored socks. I, on the other hand, snatched up a black jacket with black sweatpants and fluffy black and purple socks. I was even lucky enough to find a large brown blanket before we hightailed away from there as fast as we could. We all decided not to get the long sleeve shirts; those charity children would probably need them more than us.

"I can't believe we did that," Severin said, putting on his jacket eagerly. Both night and the temperature began to fall, making the air colder and brittle. But for some strange reason, the colder airs made me want to stretch my wings and allow them to exercise. Just for a little bit.

"You don't look like you regret anything," I said, and chuckled. "Heck no," Severin said, pulling the jacket around himself tighter. Candy started having trouble with her zipper, so I bent down to help her. As I was zipping her up, I heard her stomach growl. "Hungry?" I asked. She nodded. I looked up and tried to find a restaurant, but found none. "It looks like we are going to have to leave the park to find food," I said. "But what if we get caught?" Severin asked, looking at me like I was crazy.

"Put your hood on," I said, reaching over and pulling his sewn on hood over his head. I stepped back. "See, I can barely see your face," I said. "I didn't even know that was there," Severin said in wonder, touching the hood. I smiled and shook my head. "Put yours on too, Candy," Severin said. "It really warms your ears." She slipped on her hood. "Hey, it does!" she said. "Okay, time to go eat," I said, slipping on my hood.

We walked around for a little, checking out the stores and restaurants we passed. We finally decided on an Italian restaurant not too far from the park. The lights were beginning to get noticeably dimmer, so I guessed that meant we were getting closer to the end of the city. The dumpster was behind the building, where there wasn't a soul in sight.

"We're eating out of the garbage?" Candy asked as Severin jumped in and took out a full trash bag. He ripped it open, and the contents spilled out onto the pavement. "Yep," I said. "Dig in." She hesitated at first, but eventually came around and started munching on some rejected spaghetti. "Why would anyone throw this away?" she asked aloud. "I have no clue," I said, picking through the garbage and finding a half-eaten chicken with sauce and white cheese on it. It tasted good, especially since it was still warm. Severin was eating something with big flat noodles, sauce, and layers of cheese. It looked good, though.

Once we had our fill, we started walking again. With our hoods on, nobody seemed to give us a second glance. And like I predicted, about thirty minutes later, the city turned into two roads leading into an interstate, with forest area on the sides of the roads.

"I guess we will stop here for the night," I said as we sat next to a tree. On a hunch, I knew nobody was going to hike near us and stumble upon us. The sky was almost black, and the moon was almost nothing but a sliver in the sky. We decided to hike deeper into the woods until we found a soft patch of grass that could fit the three of us.

"Candy, I want you to sleep in the middle of us," I said as we began to lie down. I knew Severin would be hurt by my decision, but I didn't want Candy to freeze. "Okay," she said, getting in the middle of us. We all silently agreed to keep our jackets on, but I still wanted to put the blanket over all of us. Its size was so big; it fit all of us and even left out a little. "Goodnight, Candy," I said, putting my hand on her head. "Night, Severin," I said, leaning over Candy and placing a quick kiss on his forehead. I couldn't see his expression, but I knew he must've been surprised. "Night, everyone," Candy said. "Night, Violet," Severin murmured softly. I fell right to sleep.

*   *   *

Steve was holding my hand as we walked through a golden meadow, the tall grass softly brushing against our legs. The tingles shot up against my arm, making me want to squeeze his hand tighter. The sky was a magnificent blue, without a cloud in the sky. A gentle breeze blew our hair back, making him look so handsome I felt I could melt. We stopped walking and just stood there, staring at each other. The joyful look in his eyes was suddenly replaced with something much more serious. He took my other hand in his and looked into my eyes, then to my lips. He began to lean in.

Then, without warning, the ground began to shake. He pulled away, a confused expression on his face. "Violet, what's going on?" he asked. "I don't know," I said. The ground jolted from underneath me, making me fall to my knees. I looked up to see Steve, but found something much more frightening. A dark creature hovered wingless above him, a sharp-looking spear in its right hand. "Steve, look out!" I cried, but it was too late. The creature grabbed Steve by his right arm and pulled him up into thin air.

"No!" I yelled, and unleashed my wings. I jumped into the air, only to find that I couldn't take off. I looked behind me and found out why.

I had no wings.

*   *   *

"Ah!" I cried and jumped up. I looked around me, only to find trees and a sleeping Candy next to me. The sky was a soft blue, with a little bit of orange where the sun was beginning to peek out. My breath came rapidly, and I tried to control that while I thought about my dream. "Violet, are you okay?" Severin asked sleepily, sitting up. His bed hair was pretty bad, yet it looked so cute on him. "Yes, I'm fine," I said. "It was just a bad dream. Go back to sleep," I said. It wasn't as cold as last night, but it was still cold enough to be able to see my breath and sting my cheeks. "Alright," he said, and laid back down, though he didn't go to sleep.

I remained sitting and pushed my hand through my tangled mess of hair. I sighed and thought about what I saw on the television. The Dragon Kin. So there really is a classification on my species. But I didn't understand why Aaron couldn't have just told me everything instead of leaving me to make my own assumptions. And to think, he was just like me! Suddenly, I knew what I wanted to do. Once Candy woke up, I was going to try to fly to Canada and find Aaron. That is, if he is even in Canada. But, hey, it was worth a shot.

"Severin, I know where we are going to go," I said, turning to him. "Really?" he asked, his voice still soft from sleep. "Yes," I answered, "we are going to find Aaron." He just looked at me. Then he shook his head. "How are we going to do that? We can barely even fly! And besides, we have a little kid with us."

"Hey, I'm *not* little," Candy said, her voice muffled by the blanket. Severin almost jumped out of his skin when he heard her, which made me laugh. Candy popped out of the blanket and looked at me. "So we're going to Canada?" she asked.

"Well, Severin had a point. We can't really fly, and we don't know how we are going to get you there," I said. "I can dig," she offered almost immediately. I raised an eyebrow. "How fast?" I asked her. "Well, the fastest I can dig is around eighty-two miles an hour," she said simply. My mouth dropped open. "That fast?" Severin asked, purely amazed. "On average, yes." "That's amazing," I admitted. "But Severin and I can only glide, not fly."

She was silent for a moment. "Show me what you can do," she finally said. "What?" "Show me how you can fly." I sighed. "Alright." I took off my jacket and shirt and stretched out my wings. The cold air hit my body as if someone had replaced my clothes with a large hunk of ice and forced me to wear it. I shrugged off that thought and started running, my back arching in such a way that my wings were almost horizontal. Then, without warning, I jumped into the air and started to glide on the dense, cold air. I wasn't sure how to turn, and when a tree loomed right in front of me, I ran right into that sucker.

"Ow," I said as my body began to slide off of the tree. My head was hurting the most, but I think my horns must've cushioned the blow. I heard snickers and giggles from down below. "Shut up," I muttered as I landed on my butt. Severin came up to me and helped me to my feet. "Are you okay?" he asked, biting his lip and trying to wipe the smirk off his face. "Yes," I said. Then I narrowed my gaze. "If you think it's so funny, why don't you try it?" "No thanks," he said just as Candy walked up to us. "Okay, I'll say this. If you want to turn, then shift your weight to the side you want and lift the opposite wing. And if you feel like you are going down, or if you want to increase your speed, flap your wings forward," she said, her face appearing more serious than her voice. "Go ahead. Try it."

I sighed. "But if I do, you guys will laugh," I said, rubbing my sore head. It throbbed a little, but it wasn't too serious. "I promise we won't," Severin said, bumping his shoulder with mine. I thought for a moment. Then, "I will, only if Severin comes with me." "Aw, but I don't want to," he said, taking a step away from me. "Hey, you're going to have to learn one way or the other," Candy agreed. He hesitated for a moment.

Then he took off his jacket and shirt. "Okay," he mumbled. I barely heard him. I was too busy staring at his chest. It was lean, but with skin stretched tightly against ropes of muscle all across his chest and stomach. I had the strong urge to touch him, to see for myself if it felt the way it looked. *Focus!* I thought, shaking my head roughly.

"Let's do this," I said, but found my voice to be more husky than usual. I looked up to see Severin hadn't noticed the change in my tone, but a quick glance at Candy told me she had. I grabbed Severin's hand and took off running before she could say anything. My wings shot out, ready for liftoff. I jumped, and soared into the air, the wind blowing my hair back. I let go of Severin and tried to flap my wings upward. It worked! I flew higher, and now I was above most of the treetops. When one started to race towards me, I shifted my weight to my right and lifted my left wing slightly. I turned right immediately, but ran right into another leafy treetop.

"I'm okay!" I called, the leaves holding me up over the branches. It didn't feel too bad, and I thought it might be comfortable enough to sleep in. I heard a loud *thump* from my next door tree. I looked to find that Severin had bumped into the trunk instead of the leafy treetop. I chuckled and flew to the ground beside him. "See who's laughing now?" I told him, chuckling. "Yeah yeah," he said, though he seemed exhilarated. I didn't blame him; my wings felt so good to be exercising.

"That was incredible!" Candy said as she ran towards us. "You two went up to at least ninety miles an hour!" I looked at Severin in shock, my mouth hanging open. "That fast?" Severin asked her in amazement. "Yes. Now we can all go to Canada." I thought about that for a moment, my excitement forgotten. What if Aaron wasn't even in Canada? What if he wasn't going to make it? Severin saw my face and groaned. "Come on, Violet! Do you want to find Aaron or not?" He struck a point. Aaron needed me, didn't he? So what if he wasn;t in Canada? I would always be able to find him, right? I smiled, my excitement returning. "Pack up, guys," I said, my decision made. "We're going to Canada."

*   *   *

Although the air was cold, it felt good against my skin. It really seemed to bring out my flying instinct. Severin wasn't too far behind me as we flew over the interstate, so high above the ground that anyone looking at us would only think of us as large birds. All of our shirts and jackets were zipped up in my jacket with the arms tied around my neck. I felt myself dipping a little, so I flapped my wings, increasing speed as I did. Candy was under the ground, following close on our tails. We all agreed to go eastward until we found a place to stop and rest. Candy assured us that she would be able to find us when we decided to stop. She obviously had some kind of vibration gene in her, and she said that we gave off a different vibration than usual humans. Once we stopped and hit ground, she would be able to feel us when we landed. Since we were faster than her, she would be able to determine where we were in front of her. She was smart, that child.

After a while in the air, I began to allow my mind to wander. What did my dream mean? Why was it Steve that I dreamed about instead of Severin? I looked at Severin flying next to me, so close our wings brushed gently against each other. His face was peaceful, happy. Warm emotions swirled through my bloodstream as I looked at him. My gaze moved to his naked chest. His muscles flexed along with the constant lift of his wings. I suddenly found myself comparing him to Steve. I didn't get too good of a glimpse of Steve's chest, but here was Severin's, so close I could touch it. Steve's arms were bronzed and meaty where Severin's were lean, but I liked the pale thinness of Severin's. Before Severin could sense me watching him, I looked away and thought about Aaron.

I still had trouble wrapping my mind around the fact that he was the same as me. I mean, he did look pretty young for his age, and he did understand me more than the other lab workers, but I thought that was just because of his personality. And what did he mean when he said that I was the last female Dragon Kin? Did that mean, for our race to survive, that I would have to . . . I decided not to think about it.

I looked to Severin, and saw him looking at me. "What are you thinking about?" he asked. "Just about what Aaron said," I replied softly. "Oh," he said. "Do you want to talk about it?" "No," I said. He nodded and went back to flying, though I could still feel his eyes on me every now and then.

A few hours later, Severin and I agreed that we were both hungry, and that Candy must be hungry, too. We found a seemingly deserted, wooded spot where we could land and get dressed, so we landed, not so gracefully, onto a small patch of grass. We made sure we landed hard so Candy could pick up on our vibrations. "Man, its cold out here!" Severin said, rubbing his hands over his arms.

I untied my jacket from around my neck and unzipped the clothes. I tossed Severin his shirt and jacket. He pulled them gratefully as I watched. "What?" he asked me when he caught me staring, though I could tell in his eyes that he exactly what I was looking at. I blushed and looked away.

"Nothing," I said, though my voice betrayed me. He grinned mischievously. "Wipe that grin off of your face," I said, pulling on my shirt. I was zipping up my jacket when Severin grabbed hold of my hand and stopped the movement of my arm. "Let me get that for you," he said, dropping my hand. He pulled the zipper up slowly, savoring the moment, his hand brushing softly against my jacket. He looked into my eyes, and I suddenly became instantly aware of how close we were.

"Severin," I breathed, and a moment later, his lips were on mine. My face heated, and I felt an overwhelming desire to pull him closer to me. The kiss deepened as his hands snaked around my waist and pulled me closer to him. My arms crept up his shoulders and wrapped around his neck. He groaned, or was that me? All I knew was that I wanted more of him. He pushed me backwards into a tree, not once breaking the lock of our lips. I didn't want this moment to end; I wanted to bask in this hot ecstasy for a little bit longer . . .

"Hey you two! Knock it off," Candy said from right behind us. Severin jumped away from me, his face flushed from both lust and embarrassment. "Sorry about that," he said, his voice deep and husky. "Right," Candy said, unconvinced. "Come on, let's go," I said, my face hot and probably red. I tried not to look at Severin, but failed miserably. Candy rushed ahead of us, obviously eager to get some food. Severin and I laid back a little; the flying trip had exhausted us more than we thought. We both walked in silence until we found a dumpster that seemed like it would have something edible.

"I'll get it," I said, and flew up into the dumpster. I grabbed a fresh-smelling bag and brought it down to them. I ripped it open and caught some of the contents as they spilled out. "Yummy," Candy said, and started digging in. Severin came to my side and took my hand.

"I'm sorry if I surprised you back there," he said sincerely. "It was nothing," I said, though unwanted heat crept up my neck and I looked down. "You should know by now that I want to be more than friends," he said softly. "I know," I responded, and took his free hand in mine. "But I don't think I'm ready for it yet. A serious relationship, I mean." "Okay," he said, but he didn't let go of my hand. "Let me know when you are. I won't force you to do anything you are uncomfortable with." His remark touched me, and I smiled. "Thanks," I said. Then I lowered my gaze. "But you do have an attractive body." He chuckled. "You do too." We sat in silence for a while, eating our food. It wasn't as good as the Italian food yesterday, but it was okay.

When we were full, I asked Candy if she was ready to go. "I guess," she said. "Alright, Severin, say goodbye to your jacket," I said, and before he could blink, I was in front of him and unzipping his coat, smiling devilishly. "I like this," he said as he shrugged it off his shoulders. He pulled the zipper on my jacket down and took it off my shoulders. "I think I can take off my shirt without your help," I said, and yanked it over my head. "Oh, brother," Candy muttered. "Get a room."

Severin chuckled as he took off his shirt and placed in my hand. Candy shifted into her monster form and started digging. I flinched at her; I couldn't help it. She was really creepy in her monster form. I zipped up Severin and my clothes in my jacket and tied the arms around my neck. The cold was like a giant hammer hitting my body—I was missing my clothes already. With Candy underground and traveling north, Severin and I took a running start and jumped into the air, getting ready for our long and tiring journey to Canada.

Chapter Eleven

"I don't think we are in Wisconsin anymore," I said as we descended to the ground. The sky was getting dark, and stars were beginning to pop out in the darkening blue sky. We landed on the ground roughly, but with much more grace than last time. We got dressed quickly, our bodies desperate for the relief of warmth. Candy met up with us a few minutes later. "Now *that* is a much better greeting," she said once she saw us. "Sh-shut up," I said, my teeth chattering from the cold. My fingers were numb and white; I could barely move them. Candy looked perfectly fine, though.

"H-How are you not c-c-cold?" I asked her in amazement. She shrugged. "Underground is much warmer than being in the air, I guess." The temperature must have dropped a little at that moment, and my breath become almost ragged. Severin must have noticed the change too, because he crossed over to me and put his freezing arms around me. I could tell he was shivering through my own jacket.

"Let's set up camp before we all freeze to death," I said, and started searching for comfortable ground, Severin's arms still around me. I found a patch of grass not too far from where we stood, and plopped down into it.

"I think Severin should sleep next to you tonight," Candy said, taking me by surprise. She laughed at the strange look I gave her. "The cold really doesn't bother me. But Severin looks like he is about to pass out."

I looked over to him, and saw that Candy was right. His face was paler than normal, and he looked extremely weak, his hands limp in his lap. He had dark circles under his eyes and appeared to be shaking, and not just from the cold. "Severin," I asked as I sat next to him, "are you okay?" He just looked at me. "I don't feel too good," he said feebly after a minute. I quickly wrapped the blanket around him. It was so big that it wrapped around his body three times. "Lie down," I ordered him. His condition was really beginning to worry me. I lay down next to him on the grass, feeling his head.

"He's burning up," I said, retracting my hand. He looked up at me. "Violet," he murmured, and closed his eyes. "Did he just pass out?" Candy asked from behind me. "I think so," I answered worriedly. I unzipped my jacket and put both it and my body on the blanket surrounding him. "I think I'll do what you're doing," she said, and went to Severin's left.

"Wait," I told her. I unwrapped the blanket and pulled it over all of us. I was instantly relieved by the warmth it provided. "Now do that," I said. He was facing me, so I unzipped his jacket and pressed my body against him. I flinched when my body touched his; it was like touching an oversized Popsicle. I shoved his head into my neck, shivering as I did so. "He's so cold," Candy said, a slight tremor in her voice. "And to think his head feels like it's on fire," I muttered.

"Is he going to be okay?" Candy asked a few minutes later. "I don't know," I said. He was not as cold as before, but his body temperature still concerned me. "Severin," I whispered in his ear. "Can you hear me?" No response. I sighed and kissed his head. "Please be okay," I murmured as I closed my eyes and fell into a light sleep.

* * *

"Severin, wake up!" I grumbled loudly. He still wasn't responding, no matter how hard I shook him. The sun had risen not too long ago, covering the trees with a soft orange glow. Severin hadn't made a peep since last night, and I thought he was dead for a moment. A quick check for his pulse told me otherwise. "Maybe he has pneumonia or something," Candy suggested, "he can't wake up. You'll have to carry him." "What?" I asked her, baffled. I've never had to carry anything before, much less another person. Well, except for the clothes, but you get my meaning.

"I mean that if we want to get moving, you'll have to carry him. He doesn't seem to be waking up soon, and I can't carry him since I'll be digging. You're the last option," she said. I sighed, seeing her point. "What if I drop him?" I asked her, raising an eyebrow. "Let's not think about that," she said, looking away. She shifted into her monster form and started digging her hole. "Well, get a move on," she said in her raspy demonic voice.

I hesitated, but gave in eventually. I shrugged off my jacket and shirt, bundled both Severin and my warm shirt inside, zipped it up, and tied it around my neck. I took a running start, jumped up, and glided for a little bit. I tried flapping my wings, but Severin's weight kept pulling me down.

"Dammit! Come on!" I yelled, startling a few birds in a nearby tree. My wings struggled and strained to push me up in the air, but to a slow victory, all thanks to a sudden wind that helped push me up higher. "Thank god," I almost cried as most of the strain was taken off of my wings. The wind kept going, so all I had to do was glide and flap to go faster. I just hoped that the strong breeze wouldn't go out any time soon. Severin didn't seem too heavy now, but I still held him tight to me. His warm breath was tickling my neck, and his body kept my belly warm. I cast a quick glance at him, only to find his face paler than ever. "Don't die on me," I muttered into his ear as the breeze took us farther away, into the unknown world beyond. We had to find Aaron soon—he would know what to do. I hoped.

*   *   *

"That wasn't so hard," I said as I got dressed a few hours later. Severin was still asleep, but I had seen his eyes twitch from time to time. Candy was already sitting near the dumpster behind a McDonalds near some trees.

"I kept feeling really weird things above ground," Candy said as she ripped into a trash bag. "I saw some people digging up some earth on one of those busy highways," I said. "Maybe that's what you felt."

She was silent for a moment. "Why would people want to harm the earth?" she asked. "It's given so much to these people, and yet they destroy it. Why do they do that?" "I don't know," I said, biting into an interesting looking chicken thing. It tasted okay, so I ate the rest in the box. Without warning, a deep, stabbing pain ripped through my abdomen, making me gasp.

"What's wrong?" Candy asked, startled. I couldn't answer. I clutched at my abdomen as another round of stabbing pain racked my body. I screamed and fell onto the ground, moaning. It felt like someone was trying to saw me in half! I saw Candy get up and come to my side.

"Violet!" she cried. "What is it? What's going on?" She suddenly looked up towards the sky. Although the pain was almost unbearable, I managed to look where Candy was staring. Faintly, I heard the sound of a chainsaw ripping through wood. It stopped, and I felt a moment of sweet relief. Then the chainsaw started again, and the horrible pain started all over again. The slashing hurt started to move from my abdomen to my throat, and when the pain left my body, the chainsaw went silent. I gasped and clawed at the dirt.

"It's over," I huffed, tears rolling down my face. Candy hugged me, her small form strangely comforting. "What just happened?" Candy asked softly. "I don't know," I answered. I felt dead inside; I didn't want to move. It felt too good to not be in that horrible pain. Suddenly, I heard a cry from besides me. "Severin!" Candy and I cried in unison. I ignored the wooziness and forced myself to my feet and ran over to Severin.

He was worse than I imagined. His face was contorted in pain, and he was thrashing around, yet his eyes were still closed and his face still pale. "Hold his arms!" I told Candy as I climbed on top of him. Her small body miraculously managed to hold his arms down while I used my body weight to still his thrashing body. I held his face in my hands and pressed my legs into his to keep them from moving.

His cries softened after a few minutes, and, finally, his body went limp. His eyes fluttered, and then opened slowly. "Severin?" I questioned cautiously, his face still tightly trapped between my hands; my nails (close to shifting into claws) were making small marks on his skin. "Violet?" he asked weakly. I looked at Candy. She nodded and released his arms. Severin looked down at our closely pressed bodies. "What are you doing?" he asked, his voice still feeble, but a hit of a smile crossed his features. I got off of him and tried not to look at him.

"You were screaming," I said, embarrassed. "Your body was moving out of control. So we tried to calm you down." I felt the blush creeping into my cheeks as I turned to look at Candy. "She's right," Candy supported. I risked a glance at Severin and saw him shaking his head and smirking. His face was still pale, and he seemed really weak.

"What made you decide to wake up?" I asked him. He looked thoughtful for a moment, then turned to me. "I felt this unbelievable pain on my back. It was sudden, but hurt like someone was trying to rip me apart." I just stared at him. "Did you feel it too?" he asked. "Yes, I have," I answered softly. So I wasn't the only one. "What do you think it was?"

he asked. "Aaron said you two are the 'Dragon Kin', right?" Candy asked before I could answer. I turned to her.

"Yeah," I said. "What does that have to do with anything?" "Well, from what I know about dragons, I know that they have been alive since the beginning of time. I also heard that they were considered 'protectors' over the earth. That may also mean that you have a special kind of connection to the earth. When that tree was getting cut down, maybe you experienced its pain," she said simply, as if it was obvious. I thought about that for a moment.

"It doesn't seem possible, but with everything that's been going on lately, I would say that it makes sense," Severin said after a while. "It does," I said. "Though you would think he would have said something on the television to advise people not to cut the trees down."

A chainsaw sounded in the background, startling all of us. "We should probably get out of here before the humans cut down more trees," Candy said, shifting into her monster form and digging underground. "She's right. Let's go," I said, and tried to help Severin up. He could only stand for a few seconds on shaking legs before his wobbly knees gave out on him and hit the ground. "I can't get up," Severin said, a slight hint panic creeping into his voice. I sighed as I yanked off my jacket and shirt. "Hold on," I said as I walked up to him. I put the bulky part of the jacket behind him and tied the arms around my neck.

"What are you doing?" he asked me. "This is how I carried you when you refused to unconscious," I said as I grabbed him around his waist and picked him up. "Hang on to me!" I said as I started running. His arms encircled the skin below my wings on my back in a sort of hug. I sprung my wings and flew a little higher than the treetops just as the first rounds of pain struck, this time in at the base of my wings.

"Ah!" I cried as my wings snapped against my back and we plummeted to the ground. "Violet!" he cried as he turned us around with my back facing the ground. The ground loomed below us, but I could barely see, now that the pain had moved up to my head. Suddenly, we were flying again.

Or at least, Severin was. Somehow, his wings had gotten free from the clothes he wore, with the tried arms of my jacket supporting my neck, easing the unnaturally explosive migraine in my head. I could hear myself gasping as the pain slowly began to fade away.

"Violet, are you okay?" Severin asked, his voice fearful. One of his hands moved up to cradle my head. "Yeah," I said, my voice surprisingly strong, despite how weak I felt. "How are you not hurting?" "I don't know," he said, blushing and turning away. "Why are you blushing?" I asked, beginning to get nervous. Did my bra come undone or something? I looked down. Nope, it was still there. But why was he blushing? Suddenly, Severin's eyes glazed over and his body went limp on top of mine.

"Severin!" I grunted as his body weight crashed into me, dropping us a good few feet until I was able to turn and flap my wings. I surprised myself by being able to lift us up into the air. There weren't any breezes like last time, so I had to painfully strain my wings on the still air, but I somehow managed to get us up to the usual height and speed.

I supported Severin's weight with one hand and felt his head with the other. It was on fire. Again. And I think it might have been warmer than last time. Plus, his face was rid of any color it had earlier, and his face was covered in sweat.

"Oh, Severin," I grumbled as I tugged him closer to me. When will he get better? Soon, I hoped. I continued to flap my wings to get faster; Candy must have been much farther than us by now. I sighed to think of how far Aaron must be by now . . .

The sudden, strange scent of burnt metal and sulfur hit my nose, making me want to gag. I coughed and looked down to find that I had strayed from the interstate in favor of a more wooded area. There was a small bit of smoke gently wafting from a cleared, large spot nearby. I started to turn back to escape the smell when I really took in my surroundings. There was a mountain in the distance, just like the one I saw in the training room window back at the lab. Out of curiosity, I turned to go to the smoky spot. It only took a minute to fly there. The smell was so strong that my eyes began to water, but still I pressed on, a strange sense of curiosity eating away at me, desperate to find out what the smoky area was. I would only be here for a few minutes, right? After all, I felt some kind of pull towards here. Severin didn't seem to be breathing irregularly, so I decided to land and look around.

It was nothing but blackened concrete and a few pieces of molten metal standing in what used to be a wall. I put Severin down and touched the wall. Black soot coated my fingers, but the hunk of metal was wiped clean where I touched it. It was white. Sterile white—a familiar kind of white, the thought beginning to tug at my subconscious. Then the realization hit me.

This was my old lab.

Chapter Twelve

I backed away in horror, my soot-covered hand covering my mouth. This simply *couldn't* be my old lab! The lab I came from was perfect, not even a small scratch on the windows. But this place was nothing but scraps of burnt metal and scattered ash. The floor used to be a glossy white and fun to slide on in my socks when I was a few days old. When Aaron was there to watch and laugh at me. Now it was grainy and black, a cold, heartless reminder of what the humans could do to us. I touched it, and a small, cold tear rolled down my cheek and fell to the ground. I suddenly remembered the loud noise that took place when those people kidnapped us. Was that catastrophe them burning the place?

"Hey, are you okay?" someone asked from behind me. I jumped and turned around to find Candy standing there, looking all innocent in her pink jacket and wide green eyes. She saw that I was crying, and came to give me a hug.

"Where are we?" she asked gently as more tears escaped from my eyes. "This is where I used to live," I said, shaking uncontrollably, yet thankful for her warmth and kindness. She stiffened. "Was Severin from here, too?" she asked softly. "Yes, but he only lived here for a few minutes, maybe an hour," I said, struggling to contain my sadness. It was like the time those people were cutting down the trees; only this pain was emotional, which made it much harder to bear. We stood there for a moment longer, saddened by the condition of my first and, in my mind, only home.

"We should be going now. Aaron must not be too far from here," Candy said, breaking the silence. I gulped and nodded, suddenly furious at myself for crying over a place I had wanted destroyed just a mere week ago. Now I wished it was okay and running like it used to. Severin's sudden coughing jolted me out of my anger and made me run to him. One look at him and I could tell he needed clean, fresh air, and fast.

"Let's get him out of here," I said, mostly to my self. I unzipped my jacket and rolled Severin into it. He was cold, like touching ice, yet his head was heated like a desert on fire. "I think I can detect a big medical building a few miles from here," Candy said, her monster form kicking in. "It's located west of here. Keep going west and we'll get there." "Got it," I said as she started digging. I bundled Severin up and took off flying.

114

Although I couldn't wait to see Aaron and tell him all we have been through, I still had my doubts. What if he didn't survive his injuries? What if he didn't remember us? And most of all, how would he react to seeing me? I wasn't sure, but I wanted to see him, no matter what. With Severin bundled up in my arms, I flew west, hoping for the best

*   *   *

Candy was right. Within a few minutes, we entered a small city that had little more than a few restaurants, stores, a city hall, a library, a church, a small neighborhood, two schools . . . and a hospital. It wasn't very big; just about three stories high and wide enough to cover a football field. I had landed a few feet from the city border and clothed myself with Candy at my side. We had decided to walk the rest of the way to avoid unnecessary attention. Now we stood at the front of the building, gazing in wonder at what we would find inside, Severin cradled in my left arm. "Let's go," Candy said, grabbing my free hand and leading me to the front doors.

We barely crossed over the threshold when the person at the receptionist desk rushed over to us, signaling for us to follow her. "What happened to your friend? Is he hurt?" she asked, feeling his head. "Um, no, actually," I started, but she shushed me quickly. "I know who you are here to see. Let me take your friend for you. Aaron is on the second floor in room twelve," she said curtly, reaching for Severin. I jerked Severin away from her grasp, not wanting her to touch him. She didn't seem offended by the gesture, though.

"How do you know why we're here?" I asked her, putting a protective arm over Candy. "Are you kidding me? The story of the 'Dragon Kin' are everywhere on the news! I have special orders to bring you two, uh, three," she said, casting a quick glance at Candy, "to Aaron. But I really think you need to give me the boy. He's running a severe fever, and he looks dehydrated." I thought about it for a moment. Then, ever so cautiously, I gave Severin to her. "Thank you, dear. I don't know much about dragon diseases, so I'll just put him in a free room until Aaron can tell me what is wrong with him. For now, though, I'll give him pills to calm the fever. Go to Aaron. He's been talking about you for quite some time now. Hurry!" she said as she lead us to an elevator and pushed a button for us, Severin dangling from her arms.

I felt nervous, about both Severin and Aaron. First of all, I really didn't like Severin in that woman's arms; I wanted him in mine. Second, I wasn't sure how Aaron was going to react when he saw Candy next to me. I glanced at Candy. She did look a little nervous. She caught me looking, and squeezed my hand affectionately. The elevator doors opened, and we rushed out.

"He's in that room," the woman said, pointing at a nearby door. "I'll take Severin in room thirteen," she said, and without another word, she carried Severin into a room a little further down the green hall. I felt torn between wanting to follow Severin and seeing Aaron. "It will be okay," Candy said, pulling my attention to her. She smiled sweetly, and opened the door.

*   *   *

It wasn't nearly as bad as I thought. When Candy opened the door, I thought I would see Aaron like he was on the television: broken, with casts covering his entire body. But as it turned out, he seemed to make a great recovery. The only thing that wasn't normal about him was that he had a bandage around his forehead.

"Aaron" I cried, and ran to his bed. I must have awoken him from sleep, because he yawned and rubbed his eyes. "Violet?" he whispered, as if he didn't believe his eyes. "It's me," I said, my voice breaking and a single tear rolling down my cheek. I hadn't realized how much I missed him until this moment. He sat up and pulled me into a hug. "You don't know how happy I am to see you here. I really thought you were dead," he said, squeezing me harder. He released me after a few moments and looked to my right. "Who is this?" he asked softly. I looked down and saw Candy near the foot of the bed.

"I'm Candy," she said, not meeting his eyes. "I'm not a human, but I used to be." "Well then, hello," Aaron said. She blushed and looked down. He turned to me again. "Where's Severin? Is he alright?" I hesitated. "He's in the next room. That lady told us that he has a severe fever. When we were coming to find you, he got really sick and wouldn't wake up. He's still alive, though," I said, holding onto his arm. Just then, the woman came into the room.

"I hope I am not interrupting," she said. "But Severin needs immediate attention. What should I do to him?" she asked Aaron. He thought for a moment. "What are his symptoms?" "He has a fever of one hundred and three, he's dehydrated, his skin is freezing, and he is sweating and pale," she said without taking a breath.

Aaron didn't seem worried, though. "Just cover him up in something warm. He'll be all right," he said simply, much to everyone's surprise. The woman seemed just as baffled as I. "Um, okay, but are you sure . . . ," "He'll be fine. Trust me," he said. Then the woman left. My jaw was hanging open, as was Candy's. He looked at me, a question n his gaze.

"What?" "You just said that he'll be fine. He hasn't waked up yet, and you're saying he's fine," I said, shock clear in my voice. He looked at me a moment longer, then started laughing. "Don't worry, Violet," he said, his eyes warm. "You went through a stage like that too. His body hasn't gotten used to the Draki Blood flowing through his body yet. You were about a day old when we gave it to you and you got sick, but you got better within a few hours. The only reason Severin isn't better yet is because he's been in the cold." I just looked at him. "What is 'Draki Blood'?" I asked him.

"It is the blood of our ancestors. You were supposed to get introduced to it when you were a baby, then again when you were two, five, thirteen, sixteen, and once more at eighteen. You and Severin didn't get it those other five times, and that's what made you sick." "But I thought I had to get it six times: once when I was a baby," I pointed out. "Don't forget that your parents were Dragon Kin," he said. "They must've given it to you when you were born. Severin's too, or else, he wouldn't have his wings," he said.

I just stood there, trying to absorb all of this information. "But, why do we need it?" I asked him. "If you don't take it when you are a baby," he said solemnly, "you will die. That's the way it works." I was so shocked that I couldn't answer. "There is much more that you don't know yet, and that I'd be honored to tell you, but I don't know where to begin," he said. I didn't blame him; there were so many questions that I wanted to ask him, too. Like, why did we experience pain when that tree was getting cut down?

"How about we wait until Severin gets better?" Candy suggested from the foot of the bed. "I'm pretty sure he would want to hear this too." Aaron seemed to think about that.

"You're right. He would want to hear this," he said at last. I nodded in agreement. Suddenly, Aaron smiled. "In the meantime, why don't you tell me how you survived out there? It must be interesting." I returned his smile. "Boy, do we have a story to tell you!" I said, and sat down in a chair with Candy in my lap as we told him about our adventure.

Chapter Thirteen

"I know you guys haven't had a real meal for some time," Jenny, the nurse that was at the receptionist desk, said as Candy and I gobbled down our supper that night. We had told Aaron about these past two days, not missing any details. Well, I tried to keep out the details of kissing Severin out, but Candy seemed to think it was important. Plus, I decided the emotions that Steve gave me were to remain a secret. It surprised me how long it was that I hadn't thought about him. Aaron was pretty quiet throughout our entire story, but he seemed to tense when I talked about the ripping pain when we heard the humans cutting down the trees. I tried asking him about it, but he just told me that he would explain it when Severin awoke.

"Hey, slow down!" Jenny said, and took away our plates. "If you two eat any faster, you'll throw up." She paused. "I should probably tell you that Aaron will be able to leave here tomorrow. And Severin seems to be getting better, so you might be able to go back home soon," she said. Candy looked at me eagerly. I knew that the sight of needles and the smell of chemicals were beginning to make her nervous. I didn't really blame her, though; they made me shiver, too.

"Oh, give them their food," Aaron said from behind us. "They need their strength. They've come a long way." "Thank you, Aaron," I said, and snatched the plate of food back. The plate was very big and crammed with food, but I managed to practically lick the plate clean and still be hungry. "Can I have some more, please?" I asked, not just because I was hungry, but because the food tasted *so* good!

"Absolutely not," she said, and grabbed my plate away from me. Candy giggled besides me. "What are you laughing at?" I said, pretending to be angry, making her laugh some more.

"Hey, Jenny," Aaron said. "What?" she asked. "If it is at all possible, can I sleep in the same room as Severin? I know he will be a little freaked when he sees the new surroundings." Jenny thought about that for a moment. "Okay. I'll bring him in here," she said, and left the room, my plate still in her hand.

"There's a chair in the closet," Aaron said. "Violet, can you get it?" I went to the small closet and brought out the strange looking chair. It was light blue and worn, with cotton sticking out in various places.

"There's a little hatch in the middle of the cushion. I need you to pull on it," he said. I felt for the hatch and pulled. Suddenly, it turned into a small bed! "Whoa!" I said, jumping back. Aaron smiled. "We were going to get you something like that for the lab, but they're really expensive." I barely heard him; I was too busy gawking at the chair/bed. Candy pulled on my arm.

"Come on, Violet. It's not that amazing," she said. Jenny arrived with Severin. She laid him on the strange bed and went into the closet. She returned with, like, five heavy blankets and started wrapping them around Severin.

"Are you trying to suffocate him, Jenny?" Aaron asked jokingly. She smiled. "You said to keep him warm. I'm just following orders." I walked over to Severin. His face had much more color, and, when I touched his head, I noticed that his "fever" was fading away. I trailed my fingers down his cheek, making sure the "fever" didn't move anywhere else on his body. His skin wasn't cold anymore, assuring me that he was going to be okay. But I couldn't find the desire to move away from him yet.

"He'll be alright," Aaron said once Jenny had left. "You don't have to keep watching him." "I know," I said. "But after all we've been through, I just . . . ," "It's okay," he said.

"I know. You and Candy can sleep next to him tonight. I won't mind," he said, gesturing to the bed.

"Thank you," I said. "But I don't think I will fit." I climbed into the chair/bed and tried to get in with Severin. "See? I'm practically falling out. Candy might fit in, though." Right on cue, Candy jumped in and easily snuggled next to him. Aaron smiled. "There's plenty of room next to me. I don't bite that hard," he said, a mischievous smile playing across his face. I rolled my eyes.

"Dirty old man," I muttered. "Hey, who are you calling old? I'm sixty years old and still looking sexy," he said, and chuckled. I laughed along with him, believing him. "Are you really that old?" Candy asked him, shocked. "Actually, I'm sixty three," he said, dead serious. "How long can a regular Dragon Kin live?" she asked, and then blushed. "I don't mean to be rude, just curious." Aaron didn't seem offended. Besides, I was starting to wonder about the same thing.

"On average, we can live up to eight hundred years, but our bodies age much more slowly; we start slow aging at eighteen and appear to be in our sixties when we are around seven hundred and fifty-three years old." Candy and I could only stare in shock. We could live up to *eight hundred years!*

"Of course, the longest Dragon Kin to ever live was nine hundred and eighty-six years. And yet, she looked like she was about to turn seventy in human years. What are

124

you two so shocked about?" he asked us, gesturing to our opened mouths. I quickly shut mine and got in the bed with him. He was right; his bed had plenty of room.

"So, I won't age as quickly as I am now once I turn eighteen?" I asked incredulously. "You are correct," he said, putting his arm around me affectionately. "So you are going to look young for quite a while." "That's not fair," Candy said ruefully. "I want to stay young, too." "Don't worry about it," Aaron said, taking his arm off of my shoulders. "I've seen your type of species before. You can live up to six hundred years, more or less." "Really?" she asked hopefully. "Yes."

"But what species am I?" she asked. "You are called a 'moleworm'. You come from the lab that experiments with children, run by the Dragon Kin hunters. The main reason you were mutated was so that you could hunt down Severin and Violet and bring them to the lab so that they could experiment on them and see if it was possible to turn them into humans," he said without taking a breath.

We were all quiet for a moment. Suddenly, a soft moan from Severin jarred us out of our thoughts.

"He's waking up!" Candy exclaimed, jumping off of the makeshift bed and standing next to him. I rolled away from Aaron and leaned towards Candy and Severin. His eyes were fluttering against his cheeks, and his head turned from left to right. Then he opened his eyes.

"Severin, you're okay!" I said. I wanted to jump down and hug him in relief, but Aaron held me down. "Candy, give him some space to breathe," Aaron said, and got up to see him, looking like a professional as he leaned over and checked Severin's head.

"Violet? What's going on? Where are we?" Severin asked, his voice surprisingly strong, despite how afraid he looked. "We are at the hospital," I answered soothingly, trying to calm him down. He must have noticed Aaron towering above him, because he grabbed his hand. "Are you Aaron?" he asked, his voice reeking with confusion. "Yes, I am," Aaron said, a satisfied smile on his lips. "I'm happy to tell you that your fever has gone down, and that you shouldn't be getting sick again anytime soon." Severin still looked confused. I could only guess the amount of questions racing through his mind, demanding to be answered.

"What's going on here?" he asked again, looking strait at me. I sighed. "I said I will explain everything once you awakened, and I guess now is that time," Aaron said. Severin tried to sit up, but Aaron pushed him back down.

"I don't think you will want to do that," Aaron said calmly. "You'll faint if you get up too soon. Just lie there until I say you can get up," he said. For a fleeting moment, I thought he was going to punch Aaron. But Severin just glared at him and crossed his arms. "Fine. But if someone doesn't start explaining something soon, I swear I'm going to kill something," he grumbled.

"Severin, behave," I said, rolling my eyes and sighing. It has only been a few seconds since he had awoke, and he was already getting into fights with other males. When will this ever end?

"Okay, you said you were going to tell us everything," Candy said. "You are right. Let me think of where to begin," he said, and thought for a moment.

"How about the whole 'Draki Blood' thing? Severin doesn't know about it yet," Candy said. "True," Aaron mused.

"What is 'Draki Blood'?" Severin asked. "It's the blood that we introduced to you when you arrived at the lab," Aaron said. He told Severin about the doses we needed to take throughout our life. "But why at those ages?" he asked after Aaron explained it to him.

"Well, first when you are a baby so that you can eventually grow into your wings when you turn sixteen. You need it at age two, because that is the human years for a toddler to start being able to physically deal with situations, but are not emotionally ready. In Dragon Kin years, that is the exact same reason. You need it at age five, because that is the year that they usually start to get a hunting instinct. The blood helps them with that. You need it when you are thirteen, because that is the year that you start puberty," he said, and winked at me. I shook my head to hide the blush creeping up my cheeks.

"You need it at sixteen, because that is when you will grow your wings, claws, horns, and your teeth will be sharper." "But won't we need our wings when we turn five?" Severin asked. "No, the instinct to hunt does come when you are five, but the children that hunt at five are not strong enough to take down larger prey. The real strength comes when you are sixteen." Severin seemed to process this, then nodded.

"And, of course, you will need it when you turn eighteen. That is the year that your aging starts to slow." "What do you mean by our aging starts to slow?" Severin demanded suddenly. Aaron sighed, beginning to get impatient with Severin's tone. "It means that you will not seem to age as quickly as regular humans. You will be able to live up to eight hundred years, maybe more." Severin was quiet for a moment. "Can I sit up now?" he asked. "Yes, but slowly," Aaron said. Severin got up slowly. His face paled slightly, but his emotionless expression didn't change. "Continue," he grumbled. I wanted to slap him. Why was he acting like this?

"Like I was saying," Aaron said, casting a look of understanding at me. "We don't absolutely need the Draki Blood during the ages of two, five, and thirteen. But when you are born, sixteen, and eighteen, you will need it, or the consequences will be very severe." He paused for a moment.

"We don't age like humans. That also means that we are wiser and stronger than them. That is why it is our job to protect them, not because they can kill us if we don't, but because we made an alliance with them sometime around 136 BC. The treaty was created because of a meteor that hit a small village, killing all of the people who lived there. In terror, the humans thought it was a sign that the world was ending, and ordered the human Dragon Kin hunters to stop killing us and instead ask us to keep them safe from the end of the world. We agreed, on one condition; that we were to be left alone. The humans agreed, and for a while, everything was peaceful. But about three years later, Dragon Kin started to die from murder. As it turns out, the meteor that hit the village had not killed the humans, but changed them into strange creatures that knew nothing but how to kill. These creatures then became the newer Dragon Kin hunters, and that is what killed your biological parents."

We were quiet for a moment. "But why did we feel pain when those people cut down the trees?" I asked. "Actually, Candy's theory was right," Aaron said, and flashed an award-winning smile at her. "We Dragon Kin do indeed have a close connection to the earth, as we were created from the five elements of water, fire, air, earth, and spirit. When you two get older, you will actually be able to talk to the plants and animals of the earth." "Cool! I wish I could, too," Candy said. Aaron chuckled and ruffled her hair.

"I bet you do." I looked over to Severin. He looked as if he wanted to kill Aaron right then and there when his hand touched Candy's hair. I could practically see steam coming from his ears. And I had had enough.

"Excuse me, but can I have a word with Severin?" I asked. "Sure," Aaron said, taking Candy's hand and leading her out of the small room. I turned to Severin as the door closed after them.

"What the hell is up with you?" I practically shouted at him. He seemed surprised for a moment, but quickly returned to his gloomy stare. "I don't know," he said, not meeting my eyes. "What do you mean you don't know?" I asked him, struggling to rein in my temper. "I just don't like it when he touches you," he admitted softly. "It makes me feel weird." I stood there and raked a hand through my knotted, matted brown hair. "Okay, so jealousy is the problem here. But that doesn't mean you can act like such a child. You really need to—," I couldn't finish my sentence before he grabbed me and reeled me into his lap like a prize fish. I was so startled that I forgot what I was going to say.

"Severin, what are you doing?" I asked as he wrapped his arms around me and pulled me close against his chest. "I'm sorry," he murmured against the skin of my neck. "I just woke up, and I don't really know what is going on.

I just feel really weird about everything that's been going on, and I don't know what to make of all this," he said, his warm breath tickling my neck. I gulped and shook my head, his nearness forcing me to forget my anger. "Okay," I said, "I know that you don't know what is going on, but just trust us on this. Aaron is trying to tell us what we are, so suck up your jealousy and listen to him." I managed to say without my voice wavering. He shrugged. "Alright," he said, but I didn't think he meant it. Just at that moment, a knock at the door made the both of us jump. "Can we come in now?" Candy asked softly, her little head poking out from a crack in the door. "Sure. Let Aaron know that he can come in too," Severin said, almost sarcastically. I sighed and swatted at his head. I tried to climb off of his lap, but his hands held me firmly in place. "Severin, let me go," I said, but that just made his hold around my waist tighter. "Just stay here with me," he said. I groaned loudly as Aaron came in. He took one look at our position and smiled warmly. "It looks like you two have forgiven each other already. I'm proud," he said devilishly. I shook my head and tried to stop the embarrassing heat creeping up to my cheeks.

"Okay, you were telling us that we could talk to plants," Severin reminded Aaron, though his voice was much calmer than it was the last time he talked to him. "Right," Aaron said as he sat down on his bed. "Like I was saying, we can talk to the trees and animals of the earth. That is why you two felt the tree's pain when it was getting killed. The good side to that deep connection is that when a tree was diseased and needed to end its life early, its pain transferred to the Dragon Kin, allowing its wish for death to be granted." "But that's stupid," Severin interrupted rudely. "Why would a tree want to die?" "Because the trees are much wiser than anything on the planet, including the Dragons; we learn from them. They know that if it is diseased, it will spread and harm the others," Aaron said patiently.

We were quiet for a while. "What is the difference between a Dragon and a Dragon Kin?" Candy asked. "There actually isn't that much of a difference," Aaron said, and smiled. "We just tend to call ourselves 'Dragons' when we are in the complete 'Dragon' form, while we call ourselves 'Dragon Kin' when we are in our human form."

"Well, I would absolutely *love* to hear more of this insane nonsense, but I'm pretty tired, and something tells me that we will have a big day tomorrow," Severin said sarcastically, and pulled me down on his side in his small bed. "Severin," I cried as he lay next to me and put his arms around my waist in a metal death grip.

"Severin, it's alright," Aaron snapped, suddenly impatient. "I know she is yours. You don't have to shove it in my face." "What are you talking about?" I asked, my voice surprisingly steady against Severin's seductively warm body. "It's a whole male dominance thing in the Dragon world. He thinks I am seducing you," Aaron said, his voice much calmer than his angry expression, which was still pretty scary. "I am not!" Severin snapped, though his face seemed uncertain. Aaron sighed. "I'm not coming on to her, so you can just stop with the attitude. I'm trying to teach the both of you about yourselves, so I would strongly suggest that you listen to me."

It was Severin's turn to sigh in defeat. "Alright," he said after a while, returning to a sitting position besides me. I sat up, but I couldn't speak. A male dominance thing? What did that have to do with anything? "Aaron, explain to me about this dominance stuff," I said, shifting to a point where my body didn't touch Severin's too much.

"Even though we can live a longer period of time than other creatures of this planet, we are still animals, with animal instincts and desires. Dragon Kin usually travel in a pack, with a male or female leader. If there is a female leader, then usually one or two of the males in her pack will try to keep her from getting 'seduced' by another male from another pack. Severin is just acting naturally in order to keep his 'pack' together," Aaron said, looking strait at Severin. "What are you looking at me for?" Severin whined. I ignored him and stared at Aaron. "What happens if the female leader does get seduced?" I asked him. "Then the male that tried to seduce her joins the pack, or the female joins his pack." He turned his attention to me. "It works either way. Severin is thinking that I am a male from another pack and trying to join yours. In a way, I am trying to do just that, but instead of coming to your territory, I am trying to get the all of you to join mine. The human world is a pretty weird place, so I want the three of you to come with me to my own house, where you will be safe," he said, the warm look coming back into his eyes.

I was silent as I tried to absorb all of this. I didn't really think that this small group of freaks even had a leader; I thought we all just agreed that we would be going to the same places. I didn't know that I was the leader. I didn't *want* be a leader!

"Well, she has been showing signs of a real leader," Candy pointed out. I turned to her, shocked that she would say such a thing. "What? You decide on the places to sleep, eat, and when we start and stop traveling. You are the one that took care of us throughout the entire journey, and that made me think of you as a leader," she said, her voice dripping with honesty. I shook my head. "But I never wanted to be the leader," I said. "Candy is right. Plus, you kind of carry a leadership air around you," Severin said. Aaron laughed. "There's nothing bad about being the leader, Violet. Can you imagine Severin or Candy being the leader of your group? What do you think the results would be?" I considered it for a moment. Then shuddered. "You're right," I admitted quickly. "They wouldn't have survived without me." Severin smacked me on my head playfully. "Don't lose so much faith in us yet," Candy said, smacking me on my arm and giggling.

"Severin had a point about needing to get some sleep. We do have a big day tomorrow, what with us getting out of here. My house is big enough to fit all of us, but we'll need to move things around and buy bed sheets and such for you guys." "We are going to have our own beds?" Candy exclaimed excitedly. I couldn't help but laugh at her enthusiasm. "Yes, and you'll have your own rooms, too." "Awesome!" Candy shrieked, tugging on my arm. Severin's arm was no longer around me, but my side was still pressed tightly into him. I was glad for the small distance, though.

"So it's settled? You guys want to live at my house with me?" Aaron asked. "Of course," I said. I tensed and watched Severin intently, cautious about how he would react to my decision. He shrugged. "I don't care if we live in the streets or in a house, as long as we can live through it," he said, a slight note of defeat in his voice. I chose to take his reluctant acceptation as a good sign and hugged him tightly against me. He seemed surprised at first, but hugged me back.

"Thank you, Severin! Thank you!" Candy said happily, throwing her tiny arms around him and me. "Are we going to be a real family? I always wanted a real family," she murmured into the cotton of my black shirt. "Of course," Aaron said, patting her back softly.

There was a knock at the door. Jenny came in with two blankets. "Oh, I see Severin is awake. That's good," she said, smiling at him. "I brought you two some blankets for the night. Unless you want to get a separate room, it'll be a tight squeeze in here, but I think you'll manage," she said as she tucked Candy in besides Severin. I felt a flash of jealousy that I couldn't be the one to tuck her in, but the feeling subsided quickly when Severin squeezed my hand.

"Now here you go, sweetie," she said to me, handing me a blanket. "Thank you," I said, and tucked it around both me and Severin (force of habit, sorry).

"Uh, Violet," Severin questioned, "I already have, like, five blankets on top of me. Keep that one to yourself." I hesitated. "Alright," I said reluctantly. Severin leaned over and took the blanket off of him. But instead of giving it back to me, he shoved the fabric around my side. "Are you tucking her in?" Jenny asked him, her voice close to laughing. I looked away and tried to cover up my flaming face. "I guess," Severin said, though he sounded a little embarrassed as well.

"Well, I guess I'll leave you four alone until morning. I'll be sure to bring a big breakfast. Severin, do you want some food? I'd bet you are famished." As in response, his stomach growled loudly, shaking the bed. We all laughed hysterically, occasionally wiping away the escaping tears from our eyes. "I'll go and get it. Don't let Violet and Candy steal any from you, though; they've had enough," she said once we quieted down, and walked out of the room. I felt warm and happy inside, what with Severin's arm still around me, and with Candy sitting in my lap. Just the fact that Aaron was safe felt good to me, too. I wished that happy moments like these would last forever and never end. For moments like these, as precious as they are, fly away fast, leaving only memories of how they felt before in their wake.

Chapter Fourteen

"Thanks for everything," Aaron told Jenny in the lobby. She was sitting in her desk, her red hair in a sophisticated bun with a sharpened pencil sticking out of its sides. "Come again soon, okay? But not too soon," she said, flashing an award winning smile at him. "Right," he said, "because that would be bad."

"Come on!" Candy whined, tugging on Aaron's sleeve. "Let's go!" "I guess I'll see you later," Jenny said, and an instant flash of regret entered her eyes. "Well, I'd better get this young one to the house," he said, gesturing to Candy with his eyes. "What?" she asked, sounding insulted. I chuckled and picked her up. Severin was standing right besides me, his right arm still probably sore from supporting my head all night.

After a few minutes of goodbyes, we finally left that place. "Just follow me. My house is a little into the forest, but it's a real pretty sight," Aaron said, guiding us across a busy street. The air smelled heavily of car exhaust and burning rubber, making me feel a little sick to my stomach. But, hey, it smelled much better that the hospital with all of those medicines. We walked onto the sidewalk on the opposite side of the street and followed Aaron, Severin by my side. Candy kept squirming in my arms, so I was forced to put her down. "I want to walk there by myself," she said, though there was nothing mean in her voice. I shrugged, not too badly hurt. "Okay." She held onto my hand and practically dragged me with her.

Aaron led us from the small yet surprisingly busy city into a more wooded, naturally formed area. There was a little dirt path covered with a thin sheen of frost and little patches of snow. Candy kept stopping to touch the snow, the frost, and the bare trees. I couldn't blame her, though; I liked the feel of the cold, soft snow under my fingers. The trees were cold, but I could almost feel them breathing in their winter sleep under my touch. The scene was just simply breathtaking.

We kept walking for a while. When we finally stopped, Severin, Candy, and I could only drop our jaws and stare in fascination at Aaron's house. Or, at least, his natural mansion. It wasn't an average human house; it was really just a huge tree with a small gape wide enough to fit a large person through into the enormous interior. The tree was defiantly an oak, probably reaching four hundred years old and apparently still living. The canopy of leaves was thick at the top and covered with snow, making a perfect roof.

"Don't just stand there. Come on in," Aaron said, opening his circular wooden door, revealing a comfortable inside. I walked inside the tree. There was a fire in the fireplace next to the door, warming the room to a comfortable temperature and washing the inside of the oak in a soft orange glow. The tree appeared to be at least eighty feet in diameter, making a very spacious room. There was a small round bed on the ground made of straw, leaves, and a few sticks on the edge near the fireplace. On one side of the room there was a manmade stepladder leading up to a higher level in the house. The entire place was beautiful, in a homemade kind of way.

"Aaron, this place is gorgeous!" I exclaimed. He shrugged. "I guess it is. Let me show you around," he said, and took off his coat. I unzipped my jacket and got ready to shrug it off, but Severin grabbed the arms and pulled it off for me. "Thank you," I murmured. "No problem," he said casually. "Hurry!" Candy said, shucking off her jacket and throwing it on the ground next to Aaron's.

"Well, the kitchen is over here," he said gesturing to the a small shelf near the fireplace filled to the brim with pots, pans, spoon, forks, and other kitchen appliances. "Isn't there any electricity here?" Candy asked. "No, everything here is heated and lighted by my Dragon Fire. Manmade electricity harms the environment, but my Dragon Fire releases a certain type of molecule called ozone that helps the earth out," he said, looking uncomfortable. "We can breathe fire?" I asked incredibly. I was learning so much about myself today!

"Yes, but not until you turn eighteen." "Oh," Severin said, sounding just as disappointed as I felt. "Anyways, moving on," he said, leading us to the other end of the room. "Here is the downstairs bathroom." He opened the door to reveal a hole in the ground surrounded by sweet smelling flowers. "We go in *that*?" Severin asked, his voice surprised. "It's not what you probably expected, but I don't really get the whole toilet thing," Aaron said. "Let's keep going."

I stared at the "bathroom" for a little while longer, wondering how the hell we were going to survive in this place. Then Severin tugged on my hand and pulled me along with him. "Up here is where you three will stay. There are five rooms up there total: three bedrooms, a bathroom, and a storage room," Aaron said, and started climbing up the ladder. I looked at Severin, and he nodded uncertainly. The wondrous beauty I felt before for this place started to feel like a distant memory as I grasped the footholds and started to climb, Severin and Candy close on my tail.

Okay, I think I'll take that back, because the upstairs wasn't nearly as homemade looking as the downstairs. It was a big hallway, with four carved in rooms and doors. Of course, there wasn't any electricity, but the hall was lit by lighted torches, along with a room at the end of the hallway with a large window giving off a snowy white light. "Aaron, why do you have bedrooms up here? Do you get lots of guests?" Candy asked once she saw the area. "No, actually," Aaron said, and smiled. "I just knew that if I could find the rest of the Dragon Kin, I could bring them here and let them live here with me. They are all pretty young, you know." She seemed to process that, and then nodded her head. "Now, show me my room!" she demanded, her earlier happy mood returning. "Alright," he said, and suppressed his smile. He led her to the room nearest to us and opened the door to reveal a pretty large room with a window showing the snow-laden trees covering the south wall. There was a small, girly pink day bed with a light blue comforter and pillowcase on the east wall next to an empty closet.

"We can get you some new bed sheets and clothes today, and maybe a few toys for you," Aaron said quickly. I didn't know if Candy would ever be able to smile that wide ever again. "I love this place!" she exclaimed gleefully and jumped on her bed. I couldn't help but laugh at her happiness. "Candy, would you like to see Severin and Violet's rooms?" She thought for a moment deciding if she should come with us or continue jumping on her bed. "Okay," she said at last, and hopped off of her bed.

"You know, Violet, that room was supposed to be yours, but from my observations of you these past few weeks, I think you would much prefer this one," Aaron said, and opened the door to the room across the hallway to Candy's. It looked like an exact copy of Candy's room, only the window was on the north wall. But instead of my bed being girly and pink, it was a midnight black daybed with small decorative silver balls on its edges. It had a white comforter and a pale green pillow on it, along with a small closet next to it. "This is so cool," I said softly, walking over and touching my new bed. The bed sheets made it look a little off, but with some darker colors, it would look perfect. "I like it." "That's good. Now, Severin, why don't we take you to your room?" Aaron said, and led us to the next door room. It was on the same side on the hallway as mine, so when we opened the door, the window was on the same side, as was the closet. The only difference was his daybed. It was a dark brown, with the same white bed sheets as mine and a dark blue pillow.

"Like I said earlier, we can always buy new sheets and all the other things you will need." "My room is the best," Candy said, and giggled. "Can we paint my room, too? I want mine to be pink." "I'll think about it," Aaron said, chuckling. "Can I too? Can mine be dark blue?" Severin asked. "I guess. Maybe we can paint Violet's room violet," Aaron said, and laughed like he made an incredibly funny joke. The three of us just stared at him until he stopped. He cleared his throat and blushed. "Anyway, do you want to go shopping now? Although my home looks like I am poorer than dirt, I have a few million dollars in my money box. What are you staring at?" I looked at him like was crazy. "Doesn't that much money make you a millionaire? You could buy an incredibly big house with that much!" I exclaimed. "Yeah, but no amount of money can buy happiness. Besides, my parents told me to spend it wisely a mere hour before they were murdered." He had a distant gaze in his eyes for a moment. "But I guess that this can count as an emergency. Go grab your coats. Let's go shopping."

Chapter Fifteen

"Wow, this place is huge!" Candy cried when we entered the store. I think it was called Lowes, or something. Surprisingly, Aaron owned a car and actually drove us here. It wasn't a very expensive car, but it had enough room to fit all four of us (I got to ride shotgun!). There were all kinds of appliances there, from light bulbs to sinks and bathtubs. Aaron led us through the crowded walkways inside the store until we got to a colorful wall holding all kinds of different colors of paint. "Ooh, I like this one!" Candy said, and ran over to the pink section on the wall. "Oh, Candy," I said to myself, and chuckled.

"Hello, Violet. Remember me?" said a familiar demonic voice from behind me. I turned around, fear starting to settle in the pit of my stomach. There was a woman in her forties with blonde hair and green eyes staring down at me, a wicked grin crossing her features. Cindy.

"Oh, crap," I muttered, and tried to run. She caught my arm in a tight grasp and, with a powerful swing, threw me across the room and strait into a rack of paint cans and brushes. "Ah!" I cried as my wings were sharply cut by the jagged edges of the paint cans. Small dribbles of blood dripped down my back as my body weight plummeted into the ground.

"Violet!" I heard Severin cry. "Stay back, boy," Cindy snarled. Severin stopped and flinched, but didn't back away. Humans started to surround us, fear clear on their faces. "What is going on?" some of them asked. Several took out their phones and started taking pictures. "Don't worry, Violet, I am not here to kill you this time," Cindy said as she walked up to me. "Actually, I think I might have something of interest for you." She snapped her fingers, and three familiar boys emerged from the ground at Cindy's feet in an ugly smoky green vortex. Together they were carrying a large brown bag with something obviously big and heavy. "Violet, get away from her!" I heard Aaron shout. I looked towards his voice and saw him carrying a crying Candy in his arms. He looked like he wanted to run to me, but seemed unable to take a step.

Cindy looked at Aaron. "Ah, it looks like the whole crew is here. They even have a little mutant from the Wisconsin lab. How precious!" she said, and laughed. The three boys laughed along with her. Although my wings were begging to be released and to fly away, I was strangely rooted to the floor. There was defiantly something familiar about those boys, but I couldn't place their faces. I kept staring at them, racking my brain in why they would look so familiar. Then suddenly, it hit me. They were the boys that looked at me so strangely at the basketball court when Severin and I met Aaron. One of them caught me looking at him. "Hey, sexy. Remember me?" he asked in a raspy voice, then cackled loudly.

Cindy stopped laughing and snapped her fingers. The boy stopped cackling almost immediately and opened the bag. A shiver of electric heat and fear shot up my spine as he started to open it. I froze when I saw what was inside.

It was Steve.

Chapter Sixteen

My icy blood moved sluggishly through my veins as I began to feel dizzy with emotion I couldn't name. Stars began to cloud my vision as I looked at the unconscious Steve. I could feel my body sway, and grabbed the rack of appliances to steady me.

"That is . . . ," Aaron gasped, and rushed over to me, Candy still in his arms. Severin wasn't far behind him. "Not so fast, Dragon," Cindy snarled at Aaron, and right when he reached my side, her claws unsheathed and threw him across to a group of human. "Aaron!" I cried, and tried to run to him. Luckily, Candy jumped out of his arms when he was airborne, using her body weight to push him from flying headfirst into a rack of sharp knives. The humans started to scream and panic, fleeing the store and forgetting all about Aaron. He didn't get up. I turned my attention back to Cindy, my breath beginning to come faster as fear pounded in my chest. She smiled dangerously, her claws still out and sharp.

"So, you recognize him? Good, I thought you would. You see, you are the last female Dragon Kin, which means that if you are out of the way, there will be no more Dragon Kin babies, leading to the extinction of Dragons. That would actually be a good thing for us, the Dragon Kin hunters. But without more Dragons to slay, we won't have a reason to live. Unless we steal the blood of the female dragon and inject it into our bloodstreams, we will turn to dust. So I am going to give you two choices: either you gift us your blood, or we kill one of the last male Dragons," she said, and placed her claws on Steve's throat.

Horror set in my gut when I realized what she meant. Steve was Dragon Kin? I never would have guessed it was true—he didn't even have scales.

"Hurry and make your decision, before I lose my patience and kill him for something to do," she said, her voice impatient.

"Don't do it, Violet," Aaron called weakly from where he lay. "If you give them your blood, they will just kill us all anyway." "But what about Steve?" I asked, my voice breaking as tears began to roll down my face. I didn't want to die, but I didn't want Steve to die, either. My face felt cold and clammy, with my tears adding to the moisture.

Without warning, Severin jumped on Cindy's back. "Aarg!" she yelled, and tried to buck him off of her shoulders. I stood there, frozen. Then I shucked off my shirt and let my wings unleash their fury. I jumped up high with my wings to support me and kicked one of the boys on his temple. He crumbled to the ground without a sound. "Get her!" Cindy shrieked, her teeth growing to sharp points as she tried to bite Severin's hands on her neck. It was all in vain, though. The two boys put Steve down and got into one of those pathetic fighting positions you would see in ninja movies.

"Seriously?" I asked, smirking and shaking my head. I jumped up and flew over them so that I could have more room to fight. Once I landed, though, one of the boys lunged for me while the other pulled my feet from under me. I slammed to the ground with a loud *thud* as one of the boys climbed on top of me. He pulled out a syringe and put it up to my neck. I gave him a good punch to his head and he rolled off, looking stunned. I kicked out with one of my legs and hit the boy holding my feet in his jaw. It must have been a pretty powerful kick, because he literally flew backwards and hit his head on the floor. I saw Candy creep up to Steve and drag him to a safer zone where he wouldn't get hurt. I wanted to scream at her to save herself, but the boy that I punched kicked me in my ribs, knocking the breath out of me. Gathering up all of the strength I had left in my body, I was able to get up and slash my claws bone deep across his face. "Ah!" he cried, and fell to the floor and didn't move again, dark red blood gushing out of his wounds and spilling onto the floor, making a red puddle under his head.

"Come here, bitch!" the last remaining boy yelled at me, and lunged at me from across the room. I snarled, feeling my claws grow a little longer in response. I jumped up, grabbed the boy's arm, and threw him down onto the floor. I heard his skull crack on contact with the cement ground.

"Enough!" Cindy yelled, making me turn to her. She had successfully managed to get Severin off of her back, and now had her claws bared to his throat. "You don't seem to appreciate my offer," she hissed, thoroughly exhausted from her debut with Severin. "You might not give your blood very willingly to me if I just kill dear Severin, now, would you? So instead of killing him, I've decided on something different: give me your blood now, or I will take the boy with me." I looked from Severin's pale worried face to Cindy's triumphant one.

"Violet, just let her take me," Severin wheezed from Cindy's tight grasp. "No!" I shouted, my voice as raw and desperate as I felt. There were three cuts on his face dripping with blood along with a dark purple bruise forming on his right cheek. I desperately wanted to run to him, but knew I couldn't. Cindy grinned demonically.

"I think the boy has spoken for you. If you decide to change your mind about the whole blood thing, then you can find us at the Crescent City. Your eldest knows where that is, right?" she said, and snapped her fingers. The sound resonated throughout the store, echoing off of walls and returning back to her. Then suddenly, a cloud of that foul smelling yellow dust swept through the open door, wrapping around her like snakes faster and faster until I couldn't make out their forms. "Severin!" I cried, and tried to grab at the air, but to no avail. "Violet!" Severin cried, but it was a weak cry, as if he was far away. Then the dust disappeared as if a breeze had blown it away.

"Severin!" Candy cried, leaning over a broken and unconscious Aaron. I tried desperately to claw at the ground, anything to reach Severin, but the cold ground barely dented at my efforts. "Violet, he's gone," Candy said softly, sadly, coming up to me and putting her small hand on my shoulder. I barely heard her, but stopped my useless digging. I knew sobs were beginning to rack at my body, knew the tears were rolling down my face, but I felt nothing. Absolutely nothing.

* * *

"I can't believe he's gone," Aaron said hours later in his house. He had woken up and, seeing the dead boys around us, plus our miserable faces, brought us back to his house, bringing Steve with him. He had taken out a syringe and stuck into his own arm, then gave his blood to Steve. Steve was sleeping deeply on the bed in my room, his head on my lap. Candy was explaining everything to Aaron as I sat in silence, absently stroking Steve's hair, wishing he was Severin. I still felt blessedly numb as Candy told her story.

"Are you sure she said 'Crescent City'?" Aaron asked when she was finished. "I'm pretty sure she did, and she also said that the 'eldest male' would know where it is. Do you know where the 'Crescent City' is?"

"Actually, I do. That was where I grew up. It is actually a city called New Orleans down in Louisiana."

"Great," I said, startling everyone by actually talking. Excitement bubbled in my chest now that I knew where Severin was, and I knew that I would do anything to get him back. "If you know where that is, then that's good. Let's go." "But we can't just fly there with our wings; it'll take too long. We'll need to take a plane. I will buy us some tickets, but the soonest we can leave is probably sometime tomorrow. Let's rest here for tonight," he said, though I could tell that he wanted to go now just as much as I wanted to. I looked at Steve sleeping on my lap. "What about him?" I asked. "He's coming with us. We'll have to explain everything to him when he wakes up." "Okay," I said, the fiery excitement still ever present in my chest.

We're coming for you, Severin I thought as Aaron left the room to pack his things. *We'll get you back. I promise.*